She turned, and before Austin could form his next thought, she stepped in front of him. Her hands rested on his chest, and her mouth covered his.

Sweet. Soft. Potent. Her kiss was everything he remembered. All rational thought fled his mind and, as if on autopilot, one of his hands went to the back of her neck, the other to the small of her back. He pulled her against his body and his tongue explored the inner recesses of her mouth, tasting champagne. How many times had he dreamed of touching her, holding her, kissing her?

She moaned into his mouth, spurring him to deepen their kiss. The heady scent of her perfume was even more captivating now that her body was molded against his. Her arms eased around his waist, stoking the fire the kiss had started. She still fit perfectly in his arms.

Some sane part of his mind screamed, *Danger! Stop and slowly back away.* He couldn't. He couldn't stop the heat that soared through his body as their tongues tangled. He couldn't stop the desire that singed every nerve ending, making him want so much more than a kiss. He couldn't stop the possessive thought—*mine*—that floated to the forefront of his mind.

He knew at that moment that he would never really be free of her. She would always hold a part of his heart.

Dear Reader,

After *Legal Seduction*, many of you contacted me asking if Iris's sisters (Macy & Janna) would get stories. Well, in October (2015) I gave you Macy's story, *A Dose of Passion*, and now here's Janna's story!

Model Attraction was a fun project for me and I really enjoyed telling Janna and Austin's story. I think most of us have regrets regarding some past relationships, thinking we should have handled certain aspects differently. Well, Janna is no different, and when she gets the chance to make things right with Austin, she takes it. After a spilled latte, a surprised kiss and some other heated moments, Janna and Austin soon realize the passion they shared years ago is stronger than ever!

Enjoy their story, and let me hear from you at sharoncooper.net!

Sharon C. Cooper

Model

ATTRACTION

Sharon C. Cooper

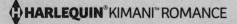
HARLEQUIN® KIMANI™ ROMANCE

Recycling programs
for this product may
not exist in your area.

ISBN-13: 978-0-373-86448-5

Model Attraction

Printed in U.S.A.

Award-winning and bestselling author **Sharon C. Cooper** spent ten years as a sheet metal worker. And while enjoying that unique line of work, she attended college in the evening and obtained her BA in business management with an emphasis in communication. Sharon is a romance-a-holic—loving anything that involves romance with a happily-ever-after, whether in books, movies or real life. She writes contemporary romance and romantic suspense, and she enjoys rainy days, carpet picnics and peanut-butter-and-jelly sandwiches. When Sharon is not writing or working, she's hanging out with her amazing husband, doing volunteer work or reading a good book (a romance, of course). To read more about Sharon and her novels, visit sharoncooper.net.

Books by Sharon C. Cooper

Harlequin Kimani Romance

Legal Seduction
Sin City Temptation
A Dose of Passion
Model Attraction

Visit the Author Profile page at
Harlequin.com for more titles.

To my hero, Mr. Cooper,
thank you for being the sunshine in my life!
I love you more than words could ever express!

Acknowledgments

Special thanks to my faithful readers for all the love
and support! You make me want to keep writing!
Much love to all of you!

Chapter 1

"I can't marry you."

Austin Reynolds jerked his head toward his open office door, where his fiancée, Zoe Davis, stood. He took in her appearance. She was one of those women who never left the house unless she was totally pulled together, and today was no different. But what he didn't like seeing was the stress lines across her forehead.

"Mom, let me talk to you later," Austin said into his cell phone, his gaze steady on Zoe. "And yes, I'll pick up the cake for you after my meeting." He disconnected and set his cell on the desk.

"Austin, I'm sorry to just burst in here like this, but I can't—"

"Excuse me," Beverly, his secretary, said, her hand on the doorknob. "I'm going to close this, if you don't mind." She shut the door, not waiting for either of them to respond. Austin had an open-door policy, but he was pretty sure this was going to be one of those conversations he'd prefer to have in private.

Sighing, he wiped his hand over his mouth and down his chin before returning his attention to his fiancée. He walked around his desk, digging deep within himself for patience.

"Why don't you tell me what this is all about, Zoe?" He draped his arm over her shoulders and guided her to the navy-blue leather sofa that took up a large part of the sitting area in his office.

She set her large Prada bag on the coffee table. "I thought I could go through with this, but I can't marry you. I can't be with a man who isn't in love with me."

Austin sat next to her. "What are you talking about? We've known each other for years. You know I love you. I wouldn't have asked you to marry me if I didn't."

Clearly frustrated, Zoe let her shoulders droop, and the pensive lines on her forehead reappeared. She sat back on the sofa and crossed her long bare legs, her short dress sliding up slightly, showing off shapely thighs.

"I'm not saying that you don't love me. I know you do, and I love you, too, but we both know that you're not *in* love with me."

Instead of denying her comment, he asked, "Where is this coming from?"

"I have always felt something was missing between us, but thought… I don't know what I thought. I guess, after dating for a year, when you asked me to marry you,

I was excited. We were finally taking our relationship to the next level. But lately I've had my doubts. We've been engaged for six months and you won't agree on a wedding date. It's clear you're not ready."

Austin sat forward, his elbows on his knees as he stared down at the floor. When he had asked Zoe to be his wife, it seemed like the next logical step, but lately he wasn't so sure.

"Why did you ask me to marry you?" she asked. "What changed? For years, you claimed you weren't ready for marriage, and then all of a sudden you popped the question. Why?"

He glanced at her over his shoulder. "Because we're great together. When we went from friends to lovers, you made it clear that you wanted to marry and have a family one day. I felt like I was ready, and I already knew you were ready."

Zoe moved closer to him and slipped her arm through his, resting her head against his shoulder. "I guess those are good reasons, but you didn't include the most important thing. Love."

"I didn't think I had to mention that again."

"But you're not in love with me."

Austin remained quiet. What could he say? If he had to be honest with himself, she was right. There was a part of himself…a part of his heart that no one would ever be able to claim. But he was in his late twenties and thinking more about his future. He had reached his financial goals and the only thing left to do was get married and have a family. Though he wanted the type of marriage his parents had, he was willing to sacrifice being in love for being with someone he liked. Austin didn't trust easily, and the fact that he'd let Zoe get this close had been a miracle.

"Most engaged people can't keep their hands off each other. Yet the last couple of months you've been traveling, and when you are home, you're emotionally unavailable. What am I supposed to think? You have found every excuse to keep me at bay. I wake up thinking about you, and you're the person I think about before I fall asleep at night. But I have a feeling I'm not the one who consumes your thoughts. Austin, I need more than a chivalrous man trying to do right by me."

He hesitated. Again, Zoe was right. Despite being ready to settle down and have a family, he didn't want to do anything to hurt her. He knew now that if they had gone through with this marriage, that's exactly what would have happened.

"Zoe, I—"

"You don't have to say anything. You're an amazing guy and I appreciate your willingness to give up your bachelorhood in order to give me the life I've always dreamed of. I know you would make a wonderful husband in some ways, but I need more than you're willing or able to give."

She placed her hand on his thigh and his gaze went to that spot. He felt nothing. No tingling. No sparks. Nothing. She was such a beautiful woman inside and out. But he hadn't touched her intimately in almost two months. Like her, he recognized something had been missing. He just chose to ignore it.

"We were good friends before we got engaged," Zoe

said, interrupting his thoughts. "I hope we can remain friends."

"Always." He placed a lingering kiss on her forehead, not surprised at how well she was taking all of this. She was independent, low-key, and he couldn't even recall ever having an argument with her.

She held the sparkling diamond out to him. As a self-made millionaire who'd made his first million investing in the stock market while attending college, Austin thought by now he'd have a wife and family to shower his wealth on. Instead, he had more money than he could ever spend in a lifetime, a huge house meant to be filled with children and a broken engagement. And the only woman he had ever loved had left him years ago without looking back.

He glanced at the ring again. "Keep it." He folded her hand around the expensive jewelry and pulled her to him. "I'm sorry…for everything. If you ever need anything, you know all you have to do is call me."

"I know. But there's something I have to know."

"And what's that?"

"Who is she?"

Austin leaned away from her and frowned. "Who is who?"

"You have suppressed issues that you have never dealt with, and I can't help but think that they have something to do with a woman in your past. Talk to me. I can—"

"Dammit, Zoe." He pulled out of the light hold she had on his arm. "The last thing I need right now is for you to try and psychoanalyze me." He'd been doing enough of that himself, especially over the last few months. As a psychologist, she had tried, more than once, to use some of her techniques to figure out what made him tick.

"Who is she, Austin?" Zoe sat unfazed by his outburst. "Who is this woman that has your heart?"

Austin stood suddenly and walked to one of the windows of his Atlanta office staring down at the busy traffic on Peachtree Street. He and Zoe might have been the best of friends, but there was no way he was going to discuss another woman with her. Assuming there was one. Okay, maybe there was.

Almost ten years now, and there was a woman who was never far from his thoughts. A woman who had walked out of his life and hadn't looked back, taking a chunk of his heart with her. The same woman he had seen from a distance six months ago and had been dreaming about ever since.

Janna Morgan.

"Okay, Iris, I have to get off this phone. I'm standing outside Cupcakes Allure," Janna said to her sister Iris. Janna had arrived in Atlanta an hour ago and couldn't wait to indulge in one of her guilty pleasures—a cupcake.

"I don't know how you can eat that stuff and not gain a pound. Aren't you afraid you won't be able to fit into one of those ridiculously skimpy outfits the designers insist you wear?"

As a supermodel, maintaining her weight and her dimensions was always at the forefront of Janna's mind.

"For the last two weeks, I have added a few extra workouts to my routine specifically for this occasion. There's a chocolate swirl cupcake loaded with chocolate chips and coconut with an obscene amount of chocolate fudge frosting on top that has my name on it." To make sure, she had called Iona, the bakery owner, to place her order.

"Well, enjoy all of that *chocolate*. Are you coming to our house once you leave there? Ms. D has the guest room ready for you."

Ms. Dalton, her sister and brother-in-law's live-in housekeeper, was actually more like family.

"She's so sweet, but I'm staying in a hotel during this trip."

"What? For three weeks? You know we have more than enough room."

"I know. Macy said the same thing about their place." Iris and their other sister, Macy, always insisted that she stay with one of them. "Though I appreciate the offers from both of you, I think it'll be better for me to stay in the hotel. Besides, I already have a reservation."

"Cancel it."

Janna didn't want to. This vacation was about more than just spending time with her family. She also planned to think about her future. She loved modeling but was ready to expand her brand and clean up her image. Being seen with some of the country's sexiest A-listers and music moguls was intended to keep her visible to the public, but lately the media had turned innocent situations into juicy gossip. She was ready for the world to see her as more than just a pretty face. If her future plans panned out, they would also see her as a businesswoman.

"So, how are the boys?" Janna asked of her twin nephews, Stephen and Trevon.

"Don't think I didn't notice how you changed the subject, but the boys are great. They're busier than ever. Not even two yet and they're getting into everything. But I love my little angels."

"Yeah, the angels that got kicked out of heaven," Janna mumbled.

"I heard that." Her sister laughed, knowing she couldn't argue the fact that at times they were out of control. "Is that why you don't want to stay here, because of the boys?"

"That's part of it."

Janna explained her goal for this trip to her sister and stepped out of the way when several women headed up the walkway to the bakery. She wore a pink baseball cap to match her outfit and a large pair of designer sunglasses to shield her identity, in hopes no one would recognize her. Today she just wanted to be a normal person who was taking her first vacation in months.

Janna glanced at her watch. "Listen, sis. I really do need to get off this phone. I've been standing out here for almost ten minutes and my driver is waiting. I'll be there for dinner."

They talked for a few minutes longer before Janna disconnected. Dropping her cell into her Birkin handbag, she hurried into the bakery, glad to see it had temporarily cleared out.

"Well, there she is," Iona crooned the moment Janna

removed her sunglasses. "I was starting to wonder if you weren't going to make it." Iona walked around the counter and pulled Janna in for a tight hug.

"It's so good seeing you again. I'm sorry I'm late. I got stuck on the phone with my sister."

"Not a problem. I have your treat ready for you. And it's low in calories and low in fat, just the way you like it." Iona winked. She and Janna shared a laugh, knowing there were easily five hundred calories in the cute little pink-and-brown box Iona placed on the counter. "Oh, and did you want your soy latte today?"

"Definitely. If I'm going to ruin my diet, I might as well make it worth my while."

Unable to resist, Janna opened the small box and licked the top of the cupcake. A sweet peace settled in her soul and her eyes drifted closed as the chocolate frosting melted on her tongue. This little bit of heaven was so worth the wait.

Janna talked with Iona for a few minutes until more customers started showing up.

"I'm going to head out, since you guys are getting busy. I can't wait to eat my cupcake." She held the box up as she turned to leave.

"Oh, wait! Don't forget your drink," Iona said and hurried to make Janna's latte.

While she was standing off to the side waiting, Janna's cell phone rang. Normally she wouldn't have taken the call inside the bakery, but it was her manager and she'd been expecting his call.

"Hey, Nelson. I hope you have some good news for me."

"Let's just say that you picked the perfect time to be in Atlanta. Philanthropist Blake Dresden agreed to a meeting with you."

Yes! Janna tried to keep from doing a happy dance in the semicrowded bakery. Instead, she retrieved her latte from Iona and bade her farewell before heading toward the entrance. She had identified several people to pitch an idea she had to start a nonprofit for teens aging out of foster care to adulthood. Unlike her, many foster children didn't have a loving family to depend on once they turned eighteen. For those individuals, she wanted them to have a safe place to stay that would not only provide a roof over their heads, but also an environment that would support them as they transitioned into adulthood. This cause was very personal to her and she couldn't wait to speak with Mr. Dresden.

Juggling her boxed cupcake and her drink, Janna wove through the small crowd in order to get to the door.

"Nelson, thank you so much for making this happen."

"My pleasure, doll. There is one catch, though."

Distracted and tuning out her manager, Janna slowed to reposition her cell, holding it to her ear with her shoulder. She pushed against the door, but someone yanked it open at the same time.

"Oh, crap!" Her cell phone slipped from her ear and her drink went flying when she lost her balance. Her baseball cap and sunglasses—gone. Trying to catch the cupcake box, she would have fallen face-first had it not been for the strong hands gripping her arm.

Face-to-face with the front of a man's suit jacket, she realized where her latte had landed.

"Oh, no, no, no." She wiped her hands feverishly down the guy's jacket until he took a step back out of her reach. Janna pushed a lock of her hair behind her ear and stood upright.

"I'm so sor…" Her words lodged in her throat and her breath caught when she met the gaze of the fine specimen standing before her. It couldn't be. "Au-Austin?"

At five-eleven, wearing three-inch wedge heels, she was taller than most women, but he still towered over her by at least three or four inches. Prior to seeing him from a distance six months earlier, she hadn't seen Austin Reynolds in almost ten years. Not since she had left Edison, New Jersey, to pursue a modeling career in Milan. They had both been so young then, but a quick perusal of the guy standing before her showed that he had grown into an extremely handsome man.

Tall, with dark eyes and chiseled features, he had a wide chest and broad shoulders, and he knew how to dress. Austin was clothed in what felt like virgin wool twill, and the jacket, tapered to enhance his athletic build, had high peaked lapels and a single-button closure. The expensive garment looked as if it had been made specifically for him. And she'd bet her last check that it was Armani. If she didn't know anything else, she knew her materials and designers.

"Janna," he finally said.

Her eyes met his, and chill bumps scurried up her bare arms at the coldness behind the one word. Not even the deep, raspy voice that she'd once loved could hide the fact that he was less than thrilled to see her. But who could blame him? One of the decisions she had regretted most in her life was the way she'd left him behind. And by the glare in his intense brown eyes, he hadn't forgiven or forgotten.

Chapter 2

Austin's heart slammed against his chest. *Janna*. Seeing her standing in front of him didn't seem real. The moment reminded him of six months ago when he had caught a glimpse of her at the grand opening of a new medical complex there in Atlanta. He'd been caught off guard then, too.

Judging by her wide eyes and her mouth hanging open, she was just as shocked. She wore that same sweet, girl-next-door expression on her face that he had fallen in love with years ago. Her big, innocent eyes were free of the major makeup he'd seen in many of her photos, and her cinnamon-brown complexion was as vibrant as her personality. Assuming she was still the free-spirited, fun-loving person she once was. And those lips. Lips that used to be so soft that he looked forward to kissing her so that he could taste the strawberry lip gloss she'd always worn when she was in high school.

As she stood there, accepting his perusal, her features softened even more. Her long, thick hair with auburn highlights flowed in waves over her shoulders, a few strands flying into her face. His gaze went lower, to her perky breasts hiding behind a pink tank top, and even lower, to her tiny waist that flared out slightly into curvaceous hips. The jeans that hugged her body like a second skin stopped at her ankles, forcing attention to her sexy high heels, showing off pretty feet with painted toenails.

His shaft twitched at the once-over and he cursed under his breath. Damn his body for responding. He didn't want to like what he saw. He didn't want to be attracted to her.

Austin tried to look away, but he couldn't. Gone was the tall, skinny girl who used to wear ponytails on top of her head and get into all types of mischief. Instead before him was an incredibly sexy woman with curves in all the right places.

Anger bounced around in his gut. How could he still be attracted to her after the way she had disappeared from his life?

Besides saying her name a moment ago, no other words formed, especially since he was fighting against some type of magnetic pull. A pull that he'd only ever experienced with *her*. A pull that made him want to move closer and wrap her in his arms. A pull that could almost make him forget the hell he went through when she left him.

His gaze went to her mouth again. Were her lips as soft and sweet as they once were?

"It's nice seeing you again, Austin."

It was as if someone poured a bucket of ice water over his head. Tension gripped his body and his heart rate picked up.

"I wish I could say the same."

She flinched, and he immediately regretted his words. He could be angry without being a jerk.

"I'm sorry about your jacket." Her apology snagged his attention when she nodded toward the huge wet spot on his suit coat, tie and dress shirt. "I feel awful."

You should was what he wanted to say, but he remained silent. Cell phones might be one of the greatest inventions, but there were times when he hated them. Had she not been talking into the device, maybe she would have been paying attention to what she was doing.

He snatched his pocket square and cringed as he cleaned up the mess the best he could, glad he didn't have any more meetings for the rest of the day.

His attention returned to Janna when she quickly picked up her cell phone, hat and sunglasses strewn on the ground around them. Normally a gentleman, Austin was still in too much shock and hadn't even thought to retrieve her items and hand them to her.

Once his mind cleared, he bent down and picked up the cup that once held her drink, and tossed it in a nearby trash can.

"I'll be happy to take care of your dry cleaning. We can exchange contact info—"

"That won't be necessary." Unwelcome memories invaded his mind, like how perfect she'd felt in his arms the last time he had held her. That was the night before he and his family had left on vacation, days after his high school graduation. And he would never forget how soft her lips were the last time he had kissed her. Who knew that would be their last time together? Had he known that night that Janna wouldn't be waiting for him upon his return, he wouldn't have gone on the cruise. They would have been married with children by now. Instead, she had left him. She had taken not only a part of his heart back then, but also some of his joy.

Austin had operated on autopilot to get through that summer. It wasn't until his parents had decided to relocate him and his brother to Atlanta that he'd finally started to move on. He'd poured himself into his schoolwork at Morehouse, where he'd double majored in business administration and finance, then had obtained his MBA. For years, he still hadn't been able to get Janna completely out of his system. Each time he saw her angelic face or that enticing body on the cover of a magazine or on a billboard, he grew angrier, throwing himself into his work. If he were honest with himself, he would have to admit that it was probably because of her that he drove himself to become a multimillionaire at such a young age.

He turned to leave, anxious to get away from her.

"Austin," Janna called out just before he walked into

the bakery. "Can we talk? Maybe over a cup of coffee or—"

"I don't drink coffee. Besides, we have nothing to talk about." He stepped into the establishment, trying like hell not to look back.

There was a time when she could have asked anything of him and he would have done it. But he had moved on. Or at least he had tried.

Janna stared out the passenger window in the back of the town car as her driver headed to the hotel, her heart heavier than it had felt in years. *Austin Reynolds.* The man she had loved since she was sixteen. The man she had never stopped loving. It wasn't the reunion she would have preferred, but to see him again stirred memories that she thought were buried and feelings she thought long gone.

She laid her head against the backseat and closed her eyes. Austin's image immediately appeared. Smooth skin the color of toasted almonds, with intense eyes that seemed to look right through her. At first he'd seemed shocked to see her, but then his eyes had softened the way they used to whenever he looked at her. His slow gaze had traveled down the length of her body, as intimate as a lover's caress. But within minutes those soft eyes had turned hard.

She hadn't noticed a wedding ring, but that didn't mean anything these days. Some men didn't wear them, but knowing Austin, there was no way he wouldn't wear one if he were married. When they were dating, he'd often talked about marriage and looked forward to being a husband.

A shiver coursed through her as she recalled how his eyes had darkened like a storm brewing. She almost hadn't recognized him. She had always seen him as a gentle giant, one of the nicest people she'd ever known, but what had she expected? Despite the fact that she hadn't forgotten him, of course he wouldn't be happy to see her again.

"Ms. Morgan?"

Janna's eyes popped open and she sat up at the sound of the driver's voice.

"Yes?"

"We're about fifteen minutes from your hotel. Is there any other stop that you would like to make before we arrive?"

"No. Thank you, Edward."

She returned her attention to the downtown traffic and barely noticed the people on the sidewalks hurrying to their destinations. All she could think about was Austin. She felt awful about ruining his suit, but she couldn't believe how cold he'd been. And it had nothing to do with the mess on his jacket. He was definitely different from the young man she had fallen in love with years ago. There was a time when he had made her feel cherished and loved. At least, until she had decided to pursue the career she had once only dreamed of having, discarding the plans that she and Austin had made for their future.

Janna sighed. In hindsight, she wished she had handled things differently back then. She shouldn't have left town without talking with Austin first, especially since they had plans to marry after high school, but everything happened so fast. Getting contacted by one of the top modeling agencies in the world had caught her totally off guard, but accepting the offer was a no-brainer. Modeling was a dream come true, and she couldn't pass up the opportunity. She hated the way she had to leave, and knew she should have tried harder to contact him once she arrived in Milan.

Her cell phone rang, pulling her out of her thoughts. She had dropped it into her handbag without checking to see if it still worked.

"Hello," she answered after seeing her manager's name on the screen.

"Janna, what happened? One minute we were talking and the next the phone went dead. I've been calling ever since. Are you okay?"

"Nelson, I'm fine. I'm sorry I didn't call you right back. I ran into an old friend." Actually, Austin had been much more than a friend. He was the man she'd planned to marry and spend the rest of her life with.

"That's all right. I just wanted to finish telling you about Blake Dresden."

"I'm so glad he's willing to meet with me." Her plans for Precious Home, her nonprofit, weren't totally fleshed out, but she hoped to at least share with Dresden what she had in mind so far.

"Well, before you get too excited, there's more."

"What do you mean?"

"He's very interested in hearing your ideas and was glad you sought him out. He'd like for you..."

Janna's mind drifted to Austin again. She might not have done much to contact him after she had left the country, but that was going to change. Now that she had run into him, she was determined to get him to give her a chance to explain her actions. Besides, she was curious. What had he made of himself? Was he married? Did he have children? A lump formed in her chest at the last couple of thoughts.

"…maybe at his place Friday night." Nelson's words drifted into her subconscious.

"Hold up, wait. What?" Janna said, tuning back in to the conversation. "What did you say?"

"I said he wants you to meet his son, who is a huge fan of yours. Junior is also a businessman and might be interested in investing. But I have to admit, I think Blake Sr.'s desire for you to meet his son might not have anything to do with your business idea, but be more of a matchmaking idea."

Janna was so tired of people trying to set her up with their sons or grandsons.

"So if I say I'm only interested in meeting with Blake Sr. and not his son, I might be shooting myself in the foot."

"I think that's safe to say."

Janna thought about her plans, which were still a little rough. What she knew for sure, though, was that she only wanted to share her ideas with people who were genuinely interested.

"You know what, Nelson? Why don't we hold off on setting up anything with Mr. Dresden?" She discussed a few more items with her manager before disconnecting.

Janna placed her cell phone back in her purse just as the driver pulled up to the hotel. She could easily get her sisters and their millionaire husbands involved, but this was a project close to her heart. She wanted to find funding on her own instead of getting them to come to the rescue. She had to show them that she could create a solid business plan and raise the initial funds herself.

For as long as Janna could remember, her sisters had been overachievers. Iris, a defense attorney, and Macy, a pediatrician, had chosen careers that helped others and, in many instances, saved lives. Though she had never said anything to either of them, she envied their selflessness and the way they poured themselves into helping other people. Unlike them, Janna had chosen a profession that was more about her, doing something she enjoyed that didn't really benefit others. Considering how blessed she had been, it was way past time that she gave back in a big way and did something to help those less fortunate. Besides, she wanted to make a difference in someone's life.

She couldn't wait to get her nonprofit up and running. Just thinking about the young people she would be able to help filled a void in her life that no amount of money could.

Forty-five minutes later, Austin pulled onto his parents' estate in Johns Creek and followed the long circular drive to their front door. His parents had purchased the house, which his mother considered her dream home, three years after moving to Atlanta, once their business started making a profit.

Austin parked his vehicle, still finding it hard to believe that he'd seen Janna. The whole experience seemed so surreal. How many times had he thought about her? Dreamed about her?

He exited the car, grabbing the cake his mother had asked him to pick up. He used his key to let himself in, still trying to shake his encounter with Janna.

"Hello," he called out and headed to the kitchen, where he was sure he'd find his mother; it was her favorite part of the five-thousand-square-foot house.

"Hi, son." Sheila looked up from pulling a roasted chicken out of the oven. "What happened to you?" She nodded toward the stain on the front of his shirt.

Janna Morgan is what happened was what he wanted to say, but instead he replied, "I had a little accident at the bakery."

His family knew Janna as his high school sweetheart. When they found out that things had ended between them, his mother had been the only one who pressed him for details. She was concerned about how withdrawn he'd become. Months later, when they saw Janna on the cover of *Vogue*, they'd put together bits and pieces about their breakup, no one knowing just how devastated he'd been. It wasn't until years later that he had told his older brother the whole story about how she had left, disregarding their plans in favor of her career.

"Oh, this is absolutely beautiful." His mother gushed over the cake that he set on the center island in her state-of-the-art kitchen. A cook's dream space, the room consisted of top-of-the-line stainless steel appliances, marble countertops and every cooking gadget imaginable.

Austin went to the refrigerator for a bottle of water.

"Don't even think about going in there without washing your hands."

Austin shook his head. How often had he and his brother heard those words growing up?

As he washed his hands in the sink, his mind drifted back to Janna. Long hair that he wanted to run his fingers through, seductive eyes, high cheekbones and lips that were made for kissing were at the forefront of his mind. Seeing her gorgeous face and enticing body on the covers of numerous magazines hadn't done her justice. The woman was absolutely breathtaking. He still wondered how he'd been able to walk away from her this afternoon. Then again, he knew how. All he had to do was think about how she had tossed his love away and crushed his heart.

His high school sweetheart, she was the woman he had planned to spend the rest of his life with. Once he became a senior—a year ahead of her—they'd created a five-year plan. It included them getting married once he graduated from college and started his career. He would work while she finished her degree in fashion. Their plan had been solid, or so he'd thought.

"Austin. Austin?"

He glanced up to find his mother staring at him, concern in her eyes.

"What's on your mind? I called your name several times. Is it work? Your dad told me the negotiations regarding that New York condominium project have been a little stressful."

Glad to have his thoughts steered away from Janna and what should have been, Austin grabbed a bottle of water.

"Yeah, we're getting close to an agreement, but it'll take a trip out there to finalize everything." As the chief financial officer for their family's company, Reynolds Development, he was used to tough negotiations. After graduating from college, despite already being a millionaire, he had joined the family business and taken the company to the next level with his negotiating abilities.

"Please tell me this trip is not going to cause you to miss the anxiety and depression awareness benefit Saturday. I want my whole family to be there."

"I'll be back in Atlanta Friday evening." He hated attending formal events, but this cause was close to his mother's heart. Shunned and disowned by her wealthy family for marrying Austin's father, who at the time was a carpenter, Sheila had attempted suicide when Austin was twelve. For years, she had suffered from depression. With the help of therapy, she'd grown stronger. Once they moved from New Jersey to Georgia, she became an advocate for others suffering from depression. It was her own form of healing.

"I know Zoe is looking forward to the gala. We went shopping the day before yesterday for our dresses. You're not going to want to leave her side when you see hers," his mother said, interrupting his thoughts.

Oh, great. Seeing Janna had made him totally forget about his broken engagement, which spoke volumes about his lack of feelings for Zoe. His mother absolutely adored her and had already considered her the daughter she'd always longed for.

"I hate to tell you this, but I guess you're going to find out eventually. This afternoon Zoe and I called off our engagement."

"Oh, no!" The pained expression on his mother's face sent a stab of guilt straight to his heart.

"Why? What happened?" She set down the large spoon she was using to stir what looked to be collard greens. His mother was the only person he knew who cooked large meals at least three times per week. "No, don't tell me. It was you again, wasn't it? I had hoped you were finally ready to settle down. How many hearts are you going to break before you understand that you can't go around dating a woman for years, or in this case asking a woman to marry you, when you don't love her?"

"What's going on?" His father, Patrick, walked into the kitchen and set his car keys on the counter before planting a kiss on Sheila's cheek. "What's with the scowl?" he asked her before turning his attention to Austin. He and his father were about the same height, but Patrick was a tad thicker around the waist.

"Your son…" Sheila started but stopped, her scowl growing more intense.

"I just told Mom that Zoe and I called off our engagement."

His father shook his head and clasped a hand on Austin's shoulder. "I'm sorry to hear that."

Austin knew his dad well enough to know what he

was thinking, and he knew that at some point in the very near future, probably when Sheila wasn't around, there would be a man-to-man talk. Neither of his parents could say anything that he hadn't already thought about. But his mother was definitely right in saying that he had to stop this. It wasn't fair to the women involved, and it wasn't fair to his family, especially his mother, who had worried over the years that he still wasn't over Janna. Before today, he was able to blow off her concern. But after seeing Janna at the bakery, he wondered if she wasn't far off in her assessment.

Chapter 3

Macy handed Janna a few more hairpins. "Thanks for attending the End Depression fundraiser with me since Derek couldn't." They were riding in a chauffeured car while Janna pinned her sister's hair up.

"I'm glad you told me about it," Janna said, anchoring another one of Macy's curls in an updo.

"Me, too, especially since you were willing to donate to the silent auction."

Janna was passionate about working with young girls and teens on self-esteem and self-care. When Macy told her about the silent auction, Janna couldn't wait to put together a package to auction off. A theme—a day in the life of a model—immediately came to mind. The winner, between the ages of fifteen and twenty-one, would receive an opportunity to spend at least two days with Janna, who would give tips on everything from makeup to personal style. They would also receive a pampering day, including a makeover, as well as a mini shopping spree.

"I'm sure there will be a lot of bids for your donation."

"I hope so. I love what the charity is doing, and if my small token can help them to their goal, all the better."

Janna removed the last pin from between her lips and stuck it into her sister's long hair, hoping they would hold the updo in place. Macy had missed her hair appointment and Janna was attempting to create a hairstyle that would show off the gorgeous jewelry her brother-in-law had bought for his wife.

"Oh, by the way, I saw that Phoenix is going to be in a made-for-TV movie with R.J. Tulane," Macy said.

Anger boiled inside Janna at the mention of her birth mother's name and she pushed the back of Macy's head forward.

"Ow!" Her sister turned and glared at her. "What's your problem?"

"Why do you always do that?"

"Do what?" Macy rubbed the back of her head.

"Ruin a conversation by mentioning that woman! We weren't even talking about actresses and you manage to bring her up," Janna ground out between gritted teeth. "What she does has nothing to do with me. I hate it when you and Iris mention her."

"Janna, you have no idea how painful it was for me to find out that even after I was grown, my mother wanted nothing to do with me. You have an opportunity to—"

"No. I already know what you're going to say. Just because Phoenix wants a relationship with me, that doesn't mean I want anything to do with her. The day she signed away her parental rights is the day she stopped being my mother. Mama Adel is the only mother I have and the only one I need."

They rode in silence. Janna hated that she'd snapped, especially knowing this was a sensitive topic for Macy. The three of them might have lived in the same foster home, but their backgrounds were very different. Iris had been fourteen when her mother was killed, while Macy's mother had been in and out of jail. She had forfeited her rights when Macy was very young. And then there was Janna. She'd been the only one of the three to actually be adopted by Mama Adel, their foster mother, after Macy and Iris had gone off to college.

"Janna, honey, I didn't mean to upset you."

Janna sighed. "I know. I shouldn't have gone off on you. I just don't want to talk about her."

For the past few months, Phoenix had been showing up at different events where she knew Janna would be. So far, Janna had been able to avoid her, but she had a feeling that the rumors she'd recently heard were true. An A-list actress, Phoenix had been approached to do a reality show, and Janna had a feeling that her birth mother might try to get her involved. The media didn't know their connection and Janna wanted to keep it that way.

"Can we forget I said anything?" Macy bumped shoulders with Janna playfully, a stupid grin on her face.

Janna shook her head and smiled. "Yeah, yeah, I guess. Let's just go in here and have some fun."

The car pulled up to the Woodruff Arts Center in Midtown.

"Hmm, there's a lot more media here than I expected," Macy said when the driver opened the car door and they stepped out.

"Janna!"

"Janna, over here!" Paparazzi called out her name, snapping photo after photo.

"Why do I have a feeling they knew you were coming?" Macy murmured. "I'll meet you inside."

Janna stopped, smiled and posed without responding to her sister. She was sure Nelson had leaked to the press that she would be there. He never missed an opportunity to keep her in the media, claiming it was great for business. She just hoped Phoenix didn't show up.

Turning from left to right, she indulged the small group of photographers, knowing that it was all part of the job.

"Who are you wearing this evening, Janna?"

"Valentino," she answered a reporter who held a small recorder out to her. She glanced down at the red, one-shouldered gown, loving the way the satin material gathered on her left side and fell in waves to the floor. She responded to several additional questions regarding her jewelry and the fundraiser.

As part of her agreement with the designer of the gown, she needed to get as much exposure as possible. She had a contract with them that stated that she would wear at least three of their evening gowns this year and so far, this was gown number two.

After posing for a few more photos and signing a couple of autographs, she made her way into the building. This was her first time at the arts center, and it was as impressive inside as it was outside.

The event was being held in the galleria, the main entrance for the symphony hall. The two-level space with high ceilings and art deco fixtures looked more like a ballroom than a foyer.

"Ma'am, would you like a glass of champagne?" a waiter walking around with a tray of long stemware asked when he slowed.

"Yes, thank you."

Janna sipped from the glass as she strolled around the open area. Round tables filled the center of the space, while the items for the silent auction were set up on eight-foot-long tables along the perimeter of the room.

"Hello, beautiful." Janna turned to find a handsome gentleman with greenish-gray eyes and a large smile surrounded by a well-groomed mustache and goatee standing next to her. "Has anyone ever told you that you look like that model?"

Janna tried not to laugh, especially since she'd been asked that question often.

"Yes, I've been told that on a number of occasions." She participated in small talk, noticing immediately that he'd had too much to drink. She discreetly looked around for her sister.

"I'm Timothy Cowden III, by the way." He placed

the glass, half-filled with a dark liquid, in his left hand and extended his right hand to her.

"Janna Morgan. Nice to meet you."

"So you are that model. You fooled me," he slurred and chuckled. "Can't say tha-that I ever met a model before. Can I get you another drink? Or maybe we can take a stroll around."

Janna startled when Timothy ran the back of his fingers along her bare arm. She jerked away from him, cringing at how creepy his touch felt.

"Excuse me. I need to go find someone." *Anyone,* she thought, and walked away as quickly as her five-inch sandals would carry her. The strappy red stilettos matched her dress but definitely weren't made for fast walking.

When it seemed she was far enough away from Timothy, she slowed and handed her empty glass to a passing waiter. Seeing Macy across the room, she headed in her direction but stopped abruptly.

"Oh, my… Janna?" The older woman's smile quickly appeared. "It is you!"

Janna smiled and accepted a hug from the woman she hadn't seen in years. "Mrs. Reynolds, it's so nice to see you," she said to Austin's mother, feeling a little awkward but sincerely glad to see her. "It's been a long time."

"Yes, it has, and please call me Sheila now that you're all grown up. You're even lovelier than I remember." She stepped back but didn't release Janna's arms. "Patrick and I are so proud of you and all of your accomplishments."

Heat rose to Janna's cheeks. She had always liked Austin's mother. Not just because she'd often told her how cute or sweet she was, but because she was so warm and loving. Growing up in foster care, she went through a period when she felt unlovable, especially knowing that her parents hadn't wanted her. But Mama Adel had always made her feel cherished.

"Have you seen Austin yet?" Sheila asked, interrupting her thoughts.

Panic rioted inside Janna. She hadn't considered that Austin would be there. When they were younger, he'd hated attending anything formal, which was one reason she had been shocked to see him in a suit the other day.

"I'm sure he would love to see you."

Janna shook her head. "I wish I could be that sure," she said quietly. Their last face-to-face hadn't gone well, and she didn't think she could take another rejection from him. "Mrs. Rey—I mean, Sheila, Austin and I didn't part on the best of terms. I want you to know that I didn't mean to..."

Sheila squeezed Janna's hand; her gentle eyes and easy smile relieved her of some of her anxiousness.

"That was a long time ago. Talk to him, sweetheart." She pulled Janna close and gave her another hug. "My son can be extremely stubborn, but you two were once very close and I think he can use a friend. Promise me that you'll at least say hello to him."

Janna nodded and they talked a few minutes longer before Sheila was summoned away.

Instead of catching up with Macy, Janna headed to

the bar. If there was a chance that she was going to run into Austin, a little liquid courage might not hurt.

Austin roamed around the perimeter of the room, sipping from his glass of scotch as he perused the items up for bid for the silent auction. He was more of a behind-the-scenes type of guy. Events like this made him uncomfortable. But for his mother, there wasn't much he wouldn't do. Besides, it was for a good cause. From the literature given to him when he walked in, he'd learned that more than 350 million people suffered from depression and the annual financial cost of the disorder to the US was mind-blowing. Of course he wanted to do what he could to help the cause, especially since their family had first-hand experience of the effects of the disorder.

He slowed as he approached the next table of donations. He had already bid on a 2009 cabernet and an abstract painting done by a local artist, but the item he was currently standing in front of totally caught him off guard. *A Day in the Life of a Model.* What surprised him even more was seeing that it had been donated by Janna.

Reading the sheet that explained the donation, Austin decided to place a bid. A friend of his had lost his wife months earlier, and their sixteen-year-old daughter was scheduled to attend prom that following weekend. With the recent loss of her mother, T'Keyah wasn't interested in prom or much else. If he won the bid, the gift would be perfect for her.

He set his glass on the table and quickly filled out the sheet, tripling the starting bid.

Knowing that Janna had donated made him wonder if she would be attending the event. As soon as the thought popped into his head, Austin's breath caught in his throat at the sight of her across the room speaking to his mother. She gave a whole new meaning to the term *breathtaking*. She was easily the most beautiful woman in the room, and the red dress that hugged her hourglass figure should have come with a warning sign—Too Hot to Handle.

"Wow, so that's Janna Morgan all grown up and in the flesh, huh?" Malcolm Reynolds, Austin's older brother by two years, said when he walked up to Austin. They both stood staring as Janna stopped and talked to a few people, even posing for a picture with a young woman. "I drove by a billboard on the way here, an advertisement for perfume. I can honestly say the picture didn't do her justice. And considering the number of guys hovering around her, I'd say I'm not the only man who has noticed."

Jealousy crept through Austin's body and his hand tightened around his glass of scotch when Timothy Cowden, the son of one of their father's colleagues, grabbed Janna by the elbow to keep her from walking away. Austin wanted to snatch the man by his shirt collar and toss his ass outside. But who could blame the guy for buzzing around her like a moth drawn to a flame when she looked that hot? Besides the fact she was dressed to the nines, her hair was piled haphazardly on top of her head with a few tendrils framing her face, making her look sexier than any woman had the right to look. And then she smiled. Damn, he'd missed that smile that lit up her entire face.

Frustration coursed through his veins and he glanced away, mentally shaking himself. He wanted to be mad at her, wanted to hate her for the way she left him without as much as a note or telephone call. The last thing he should be doing was standing there, salivating over how amazing she looked and remembering how much her smile once affected him.

When his gaze returned to where she was standing, he watched as she pulled away from Timothy, her long, graceful stride taking her to the bar.

"I know you still have some issues that you haven't dealt with when it comes to her, but if I were you—"

"Well, you're not me, so you can just keep your thoughts and opinions to yourself."

"Touchy, touchy."

"I need another drink." Austin walked away, ignoring his brother's laughter.

It's going to be a long night.

Austin walked up to the bar, where Janna was now standing. Her intoxicating scent of roses and baby powder sent a jolt of awareness to a certain part of his body.

"Hello, Janna," he said when she glanced at him, surprise in her eyes. Just as quick, something else showed. Fear? Regret? Whatever it was, he was sure it had everything to do with the way he had treated her the other day. Instead of apologizing for his rudeness, he said, "Can I get you something else to drink?" He nodded at the semi-empty glass in her hand.

"Are you sure you want to do that? The last time I was near you and had a drink in my hand, it didn't end well," she said, the sultriness of her voice a reminder that she was all grown up now.

He chuckled. "I'll take my chances. What would you like?"

"Ginger ale." Austin lifted an inquiring eyebrow. "Two alcoholic drinks, which I have already consumed, is my limit."

"I see." He turned to the bartender and placed their order.

Silence loomed while they waited for their drinks, and Austin's gaze lingered to her right hand resting on the bar. The promise-me ring with the small diamond he'd given her was on her middle finger. He had worked months, saving every penny in order to purchase it before her special day. He couldn't believe she still had it, let alone was wearing the jewelry.

He still recalled the day, her sixteenth birthday. He had taken her on a picnic in Roosevelt Park in Edison, New Jersey. The memory made him smile. It was a beautiful autumn day when the leaves on the trees were starting to change and the air was a little crisp. They'd sat huddled together near the gazebo overlooking Meadow Lake as he fed her fruit and entertained her with corny jokes, loving the fact that she'd laughed at all of them. That was also the day he had proposed marriage to her, as only a seventeen-year-old boy could do.

Austin shook his head, hoping to rid his mind of the unwelcome thoughts. He didn't want to think about the absurdity of proposing at that age. And now realizing he had proposed marriage twice, to two different women, in the last ten years made him feel like an incompetent loser. Sure, Janna and Zoe had accepted, but he still hadn't been able to close the deal with either, which in hindsight was lucky for him. Clearly he had a problem making good decisions when it came to matters of the heart.

"Here you go." The bartender placed the drinks in front of them.

"Thank you." Janna lifted her glass to Austin in a silent toast before taking a sip.

"My pleasure."

Austin took a long drag on his beer, hoping the bitter liquid would tamp down his desire to question her decision to leave him years ago. He wasn't sure if he was ready for her response, but a part of him needed to know.

"I like a woman who plays hard to get," Timothy slurred when he saddled up to the other side of Janna. She rolled her eyes and groaned, moving slightly closer to Austin, but Timothy was not to be ignored. "I don't give up easy." He dropped his arm around her shoulder.

Austin's protective instincts kicked in and he almost grabbed Timothy, but he stopped himself. Janna was no longer his responsibility. He kept quiet, hoping Timothy didn't go further than a little flirting.

"What part of 'I'm not interested' don't you understand?" she ground out only loud enough for those right next to them to hear. She shook his arm loose. "Besides, I'm already with someone."

She turned, and before Austin could form his next thought, she stepped in front of him. Her hands rested on his chest, and her mouth covered his.

Sweet. Soft. Potent. Her kiss was everything he remembered. All rational thought fled his mind and, as if on autopilot, one of his hands went to the back of her neck, the other to the small of her back. He pulled her against his body and his tongue explored the inner recesses of her mouth, tasting champagne. How many times had he dreamed of touching her, holding her, kissing her?

She moaned into his mouth, spurring him to deepen their kiss. The heady scent of her perfume was even more captivating now that her body was molded against his. Her arms eased around his waist, stoking the fire the kiss had started. She still fit perfectly in his arms.

Some sane part of his mind screamed, *Danger! Stop and slowly back away.* He couldn't. He couldn't stop the heat that soared through his body as their tongues tangled. He couldn't stop the desire that singed every nerve ending, making him want so much more than a kiss. He couldn't stop the possessive thought—*mine*— that floated to the forefront of his mind.

He knew at that moment that he would never really be free of her. She would always hold a part of his heart.

Janna's heartbeat thumped faster when Austin's large hands moved from her body and cupped her face. She might have started the kiss, but with the demanding mastery of his lips, he had quickly taken charge. His fresh, clean scent was more potent than the alcohol on his tongue.

That peace she'd always felt in his presence settled over her like a soft silk-wool sweater. God, she had missed him. His closeness, his warmth and his hands on her felt so familiar. Like old times.

She heard herself moan.

His body stiffened.

Her heart lurched, and the wistful murmurs from people nearby penetrated the fog in her head caused by the toe-curling kiss. The last thing she wanted to do was open her eyes, but then she heard what sounded like a camera.

Her eyes flew open.

Oh, crap.

If Austin had hated her before, the scathing look in his dark eyes now said that he was beyond angry.

"Let's go," he growled under his breath and held her elbow, guiding them through the small crowd that had gathered. He pulled her along, using his large body to block their faces from any additional photographs, and didn't stop moving until they were outside. "What the hell was that all about?"

"Austin, I'm sorry. I'm so sorry. I didn't think—"

"Yeah, that's the problem, Janna. You never think about how your actions are going to affect someone else. You're still the selfish, careless, impulsive person you were years ago."

Fury rumbled inside her and she placed her hands on her hips, stepping closer to him.

"Now, you wait just a minute! You have every right to be mad at me for kissing you, but I will not stand here and let you call me names. You don't know me!"

"And whose fault is that?"

Janna stared at him. Hurt flickered in his eyes, but

disappeared so quickly she thought she might have imagined it. Guilt churned in her gut. He wasn't only talking about tonight. Tension bounced off him like heat from a roaring fire as she struggled for the right words to say. So many times she had imagined what she would say to him when she had a chance to apologize. Yet nothing seemed to be good enough.

"Austin, listen."

"No, you listen. I don't know what that kiss was all about back there, but count me out of any games that you're playing. You gave up your rights to kiss me on a whim years ago. Now stay the hell away from me."

Instead of going back to the event, he stormed away along the concrete path that led around the building.

Remorse settled in her chest. She and Austin had once been so good together. He was her first love. The first person outside of Mama Adel who'd made her feel special. She had vowed back then to love him forever. Instead, she had discarded their plans for the first opportunity for fame and fortune that had come her way.

Janna toyed with the promise ring that went everywhere she did. She knew now that Austin would never listen to anything she had to say. He would never forgive her.

Chapter 4

Two days later, Austin sat in a meeting, half listening to the weekly report from department heads. Due to traveling, he had already missed two meetings that month and needed to be brought up to date, but he couldn't focus. He couldn't shake the confusing emotions left behind by that kiss Janna had planted on him. It might have been unexpected, but he would be lying if he said that he hadn't enjoyed finding out that her lips were still cushiony soft. But damn his treacherous body for wanting more than a kiss from her.

"We've had to hire a different carpenter contractor for the San Jose project." Clarence Golding, the project director, cut into Austin's thoughts. "The one we were using is under a federal investigation, and no, it has nothing to do with Reynolds Development," he said, as if knowing Austin or his father would ask.

"That's good to know." Patrick stood and walked across the room, pouring himself another cup of coffee. "How are things with..."

Austin's mind drifted again as he stared out the conference room window, exhaustion consuming his body. He hadn't had a good night's sleep since the fundraiser. Flashbacks of the way he had spoken to Janna continued to trouble him. There was a time when he wouldn't have even considered raising his voice to her or uttering a mean word. And after he'd told her to stay away from him, the night had gone downhill from there. He had intended to leave the event early but not before the dinner. Of course, the first call he received Sunday morning was from his mother. To say she was pissed would be an understatement. But she'd definitely gotten his attention when she pointed out his recent failures where women were con—

"Is everything all right, son?"

Austin's gaze lifted to where his father stood near the chair at the head of the conference table, staring at him, concern in his eyes. Glancing around, Austin was surprised to see that everyone else had cleared out.

He closed the file in front of him and stood. "Yes, sir, everything is fine."

"Then why have you been distracted since you arrived this morning? This is our third meeting of the day and you have only interjected maybe once or twice. Normally on a Monday morning, you're full of information, bringing us all up to date on the financials for each project."

Austin gathered his files and pen. "Sorry, Dad. I guess I just have a lot on my mind."

"Does your lack of focus have anything to do with this?" Patrick unfolded a newspaper and dropped it in front of Austin. "Looks like you put on quite the show Saturday night. I'm not sure how your mother and I missed this."

Austin groaned and picked up the newspaper, zoning in on the picture of him and Janna kissing.

Catwalk Queen Has a New Beau was splashed across the top of the article.

Janna Morgan has been on the arms of many leading men, music moguls and professional athletes, but this is the first time she's been caught kissing anyone. According to our sources, the mystery man is an Atlanta business executive, Austin Reynolds. Is Reynolds just another notch in the model's designer belt, or could this be more serious?

Austin quickly skimmed the rest of the article as anger simmered within him. For almost twenty-eight years he'd managed to stay clear of any negative publicity, and Janna showed up in town and suddenly he was top entertainment news.

Cursing under his breath, he dropped the paper on the table. How should he handle this? If he kept quiet, maybe it would just go away.

"I didn't realize you two had reunited. I spoke briefly with Janna Saturday night and she's as sweet as I remember, but she didn't lead me to believe that you two were back together."

"That's because we're not. That...that," he stuttered and pointed at the photo, "shouldn't have happened."

"Well, you can't tell by looking at the picture." His father chuckled. "As a matter of fact, if I didn't know any better, I would think you two were very much in love. A man doesn't kiss a woman like that unless he still has feelings for her."

Austin didn't want to have this conversation. It had taken him weeks after Janna had left for him to even tell his parents that she'd gone to Italy to pursue a modeling career. And even then the only thing he'd told them was that they weren't together anymore.

"Well, this is a good example of the media getting it all wrong." Austin made a move to leave but stopped when his father called his name.

"When will I have the numbers for the Dunkin project in Alpharetta?"

Patrick and his brother had built the company from the ground up and within five years had made it into a million-dollar business. While in college, Austin had interned for his father, working six days a week while carrying a full class load. He had always had business sense, even from a very young age, and had been good with numbers. His father had groomed him to one day fill the role of chief financial officer. His BA in business and finance, as well as his MBA, enhanced what he had learned on the job.

"I had planned to have that information to you this morning, but you'll definitely have it on your desk before I leave today."

Austin got to the closed conference room door before his father spoke again.

"Son, I know it's none of my business, but when are you going to let the past go?" He nodded toward the newspaper. "It's clear you two have some unfinished business. And I have watched you the last few years, getting in and out of relationships, looking for something you apparently haven't found. Is it possible that you've been looking in the wrong place? Maybe Janna is what's missing in your life."

"Dad."

"Hear me out." His father grabbed the newspaper from the table and refolded it, sticking it in the file that was in his hand. "There's nothing I want more than for you and your brother to find women who will make you as happy as your mother has made me. But there's something you need to understand. Getting hurt is a part of life. Staying hurt is a choice."

Austin stood stunned. His father was an intelligent man, a man he'd always looked up to. Hearing him go deep on him was a new experience, though.

"You are never going to find what you're looking for until you deal with whatever happened between you and Janna. You're also not going to find it if you continue to spend every waking hour here at the office or holed up in your workshop."

When most people went home to their families or out for drinks after work, Austin spent his spare time at home in his workshop. Since he was a kid, he'd loved working with wood and as an adult built cabinets and chests in his spare time.

"Search your heart and reevaluate your priorities. I guarantee you'll get the life you long for."

Silence fell between them until Austin asked, "So when did you know Mom was the one?"

His father chuckled. "The first time I kissed her. From that moment on, she was the first person I thought of when I woke up each day and the last person I thought of before I fell asleep each night."

A sick feeling swirled around inside Austin's chest. Hearing the same words Zoe had spoken made him realize that he hadn't thought about her all weekend. *What the heck?* How could he have planned to marry someone whom he could forget that easily? The day before the fundraiser, she had flown to Tampa to check on her mother, who had taken a fall.

Shaking his head, he followed Patrick out of the conference room.

"I'm sorry things didn't work out with you and Zoe, but in a way, maybe it was a blessing in disguise," his father said before he headed down the hall toward his office.

Austin stared after him before returning to his own office, feeling the weight of his father's words. He was right about one thing. It was time Austin put the past in the past. But how could he? Each time he saw Janna, the hurt she'd caused came back to him as if it had happened yesterday.

Austin placed the files on his desk and dropped into

his chair, his head in his hands. Janna came crashing back into his life as only she could do. He shook his head, unable to stop the smile that came with the thought. Even without trying, she had shaken up his world as she used to do. He had always been a slave to routine and normalcy, while she was the opposite. There was never anything normal about their time together. Either she was doing something that would eventually get them into trouble, or she was trying to loosen him up. Her words, not his. That was something he had loved about having her in his life. She made him want to live out loud instead of living in a nice, neat and simple existence.

Austin lifted his head and sat back in his seat. Thinking of Janna was only going to make him frustrated. He could forgive her for leaving him in New Jersey, but he didn't know if it were possible to forget.

"Thank you," Janna said to the driver holding the door as she climbed into the back of the town car. It felt as if she'd put in a full day of work arguing with the owner of the management company that handled her finances. She couldn't believe that the accountant assigned to oversee one of her smaller retirement accounts had mishandled her funds. For years, Iris had told her she needed to learn everything she could about how they were managing her money or at least learn how to read the monthly reports they sent her. Janna had finally decided to do just that.

She had started making money so fast that she hadn't kept up very well in how her finances were being managed. And though she would hate admitting this to any-one, she'd been too busy to keep track of the money coming in and going out lately.

Her brother-in-law, Nash, planned to give her the contact information to his accountant as well as a crash course in finance, while Iris looked into crimi-nal charges.

Seeing how backed up the traffic was, Janna sat back and got comfortable for the ride to Nash's office.

Janna's cell phone rang and she wondered if that was Nash calling to make sure she was still stopping by his office.

"Hello," she said once she located her cell phone at the bottom of her handbag.

"For a person who is trying to clean up her image, you have a funny way of showing it," Iris said.

Janna rolled her eyes. She had hoped no one she knew saw the photo and the article, but the call from Macy the day before proved otherwise.

"Hey, Auntie Janna! Nice photo!" Iris's daughter screamed in the background. When Iris met Nash, he'd been raising Tania, his niece, by himself. He and Iris officially adopted her after they were married.

"Tell Tania she's not funny. And tell her that I want to see her before I leave Atlanta."

"That's going to be a little hard, since I'm taking her and one of her girlfriends to the airport as we speak. They're starting their summer vacation in South Beach."

"I can't believe Nash is letting her go there by her-self," Janna said, knowing how overprotective her brother-in-law could be.

"Trust me, it wasn't easy. She had to remind him that she's an adult now. But enough about Tania. Let's talk about you and that photo."

"Go ahead. Get it out your system. Let me have it," she said to her sister. "I knew it was only a matter of time before I heard from you." Janna glanced at her watch.

"It is such a small world," Iris said. "I had no idea you knew Austin Reynolds."

"What are you talking about? I told you and Macy about Austin years ago. He's the one who gave me the promise ring." She glanced down at her hand. Iris was eight years older than her and Macy was ten years older. Both had gone off to college before Janna made it to high school.

"That was him?" Iris's voice rose. "I can't believe *Austin Reynolds* gave you a promise ring. I didn't even realize he grew up in New Jersey."

"You act as if he's someone famous." Janna had done a little research on him after the disaster at the fundraiser. She wasn't surprised to learn that he was the CFO of his family's business and had won Atlanta's businessman of the year award a couple of years ago, making him the youngest recipient in the history of the award. She'd always known he would be successful at whatever he set his mind to.

"He might not be famous, but if you're serious about changing your image, you kissed the right person Saturday night."

Apparently, Macy had filled Iris in on some of the details of what happened.

"I didn't kiss him with some ulterior motive, except...
I guess I sorta did. I was trying to dissuade this other
guy's advances and I went too far. But there is no way I
would use Austin."

"I'm not saying you're trying to use him. I guess
what I should have said is that Austin is Atlanta's golden
child."

"What do you mean?"

"It started when Austin was attending Morehouse.
He stopped a mugger from getting away with a city
councilwoman's handbag. She dubbed him a hero and
shared the story with anyone who would listen. During his college years, he had also spearheaded some
major community projects, raising most of the money
on his own." Iris filled her in on one instance after another, including how, a year ago, he had donated a four-
story building to an organization that worked with the
homeless.

"Okay, okay, you're right. He's a saint. And now
thanks to me, he's in the paper in a less-than-favorable
manner. God, I feel awful." Janna rubbed her temples.
He'd already hated her. There probably wasn't a word
that could describe what he thought of her now. "So
how do you know so much about him?" she asked Iris.

"His company has done a lot of work for Nash over
the years, and now he's good friends with Austin and
his family."

"I can't believe what I did to him."

"Janna, I think you're being too hard on yourself.
There's not a guy alive who wouldn't have killed to be

in Austin's shoes Saturday night. If anything, you've made him the most envied man in town."

"Yeah, but Austin doesn't like attention, especially not that type. I had hoped that while I was in Atlanta I could make things right between us. I'm sure his feelings for me aren't what they used to be back in New Jersey, but I wanted to, to…oh, hell, I don't know what I was hoping for."

"You were hoping he still had feelings for you the way you clearly still care for him," Iris said without missing a beat.

Janna more than cared for Austin. There hadn't been a day that went by that she didn't think about him. She had written him a letter prior to leaving the country but never heard from him. Of course he would have been disappointed that she was putting a modeling opportunity before their relationship, but she had hoped that he would have at least acknowledged the letter. Now she would never get the chance to find out why he'd never responded.

"I heard you let some young punks beat you on the basketball court last week," Austin said to Nash Dupree and took a long gulp of his sweet tea. They were lounging in Nash's office discussing the budget for his latest project. As the owner of several nightclubs in Atlanta, Nash had contracted Austin's company to build an addition onto one of his buildings.

"I'm not going to even ask where you heard that, or maybe I should say who you heard it from. I'm sure it was Big Mouth Nigel who's spreading those vicious rumors."

Austin laughed. "I can't reveal my sources, but just so you know, it's more than just rumor. There's a video."

Nash groaned. "Damn. I need to find the person who is responsible for having cameras on these damn cell phones. Is nothing private these days?"

Austin's grin slowly slipped from his lips. He'd wondered the same thing, thinking about the photo of him and Janna. Days after the searing kiss, it was as if he could still feel her lips against his.

"You know I have to ask, don't you?"

Austin cocked an eyebrow. "Ask what?"

"How do you know Janna Morgan?"

"Man, not you, too." Austin set his almost empty glass on the coaster in front of him and stood, rubbing the back of his neck.

"Hey, I'm not trying to get all in your business. I was just wondering because she's my sister-in-law."

Austin whirled around. "What?"

Nash grinned and walked around to the front of his desk, sitting on the edge of it. He folded his arms across his chest.

"Yep."

Austin's mind took him back to when he and Janna dated. She had often mentioned having two sisters, but he had never met them.

"So Iris is her sister?"

Nash nodded.

"I had no idea. Damn. Talk about a small world."

"It sure is. Imagine my surprise when Iris showed

me the article in the newspaper. We didn't know you and Janna knew each other. And by the looks of the picture, I'd say you guys know each other very well."

He and Nash had associated outside of business, but the subject of him being related to a supermodel had never come up.

"We went to school together," Austin finally said.

"So do you kiss all of your old classmates like that?"

Austin shook his head and chuckled. *Hell, no* were the first words that came to mind. As a matter of fact, he hadn't even experienced a kiss like that with his ex-fiancée. A kiss that had rocked his world and turned it on its axis.

"No. Janna and I dated for a couple of years in high school. Until this past week, I hadn't seen her in almost ten years."

"Well, damn, man. If that's how you two say, *hello, long time no see*, I don't want to think about how you guys greeted each other back then."

"Let's just say your sister-in-law is as unpredictable as I remember. That kiss was definitely not something I planned."

He told Nash about how Timothy had been coming on to her and how she initiated the kiss.

Nash stood and stuffed his hands into his pockets. "Actually, that sounds like Janna. We knew each other before I met Iris."

Unease traveled through Austin's body. There was a time when Nash had been considered one of the country's most eligible bachelors, as well as a man who had his pick of women. The thought of him and Janna together didn't sit well with Austin.

"Hold up, man," Nash said as if reading Austin's mind. "Before you let your imagination get carried away, nothing happened between us."

"I didn't say anything."

"You didn't have to. The daggers shooting from your eyes said it all. Janna and I attended a few movie premieres together. Each time was business and always platonic."

"Hey, you don't have to explain anything to me. I have no claims on her. What we had was a long time ago."

Nash gave him a look as if to say he didn't believe him. "All right, man. If you say so." He moved to the other side of the desk when his cell phone chirped.

Austin glanced at his watch, noting that it was after six. He hadn't planned on staying as long as he had.

"If you need to take that call, I can head out. We've covered everything regarding the club in Midtown."

"Actually, it's just a text. Give me a second." Nash typed something quickly and set the phone down. "Okay, sorry about that. As for the Midtown location, I know this is going to jack up the cost, but I think I want that back room sectioned off. And instead of all carpet in that space, I want travertine floors on the other side of the sitting area."

They talked for minutes longer and Austin added a few notes on his iPad, promising to forward the information to the supervisor assigned to the job.

"I'll work the numbers and get back to you next week," Austin told him, preparing to leave.

"That'll be good."

Someone knocked on Nash's office door.

"Come in," he called out.

The door swung open and Austin's breath caught in his throat. His surprise quickly turned to anger.

"Are you stalking me?" he said between clenched teeth.

"What?" Janna's hands flew to her narrow hips and she glared at him.

"You heard me. Why is it that everywhere I go, you show up?" Austin wasn't sure what to think. Part of him wanted to be anywhere she wasn't, but another part of him came alive whenever she was near.

"You know what, Austin?" Janna started.

Nash cleared his throat. "I think I need to check on something downstairs." He left them standing in the middle of the room, glaring at each other.

"Stop looking at me like that! I'm not stalking you. I came to talk to Nash about something. Had I known you'd be here, I would have stopped by another time."

He studied her. Her ponytail rested over her shoulder, reminding him of their high school days. He liked it hanging off to the side the way it was now. It made her look cute and carefree, like the girl he'd fallen in love with all those years ago.

His gaze went to her full lips, painted a mauve-like color. He couldn't help but remember their softness and how good they felt against his.

Apparently he was a glutton for punishment, because damn if he didn't want to kiss her again.

Chapter 5

"Look, Austin. I can't apologize enough for Saturday night. I would never intentionally put you in that type of situation. You were right. I'm still impulsive. Unfortunately, that's probably never going to change."

Austin turned from Janna and ran his hand over his head, letting it slide down to the back of his neck. One of his biggest regrets about Saturday night was how he had spoken to her.

He turned back to her and their eyes met. "I'm sorry, too. I shouldn't have talked to you the way I did."

Though he'd meant what he said, he hated the way he'd said it. Even if they were no longer a couple, he wouldn't want anyone to treat her the way he had that night.

Austin's gaze followed her every move, appreciating how good she looked in a simple multicolored sundress that tied behind her neck and sky-high sandals that matched the color of her lips.

She glided the short distance to Nash's leather sofa and set her large purse down on the table in front of it. She turned in time to catch him staring. He couldn't look away even if he wanted. Longing rocked his entire being. There was just something about her. Something about the way the air shifted when she stepped into a room. Something about the way his body hummed whenever she was near. Something about the way his heart rate kicked up whenever she looked at him with those big, bright, sexy eyes, the way she was doing now.

He mentally shook himself and forced his gaze away.

"In regards to your accusation about me stalking you, I had no idea you were here. But you have to admit, our meeting like this must be fate. We've run into each other three times within a week."

Austin chanced a glance at her. He wasn't sure if it were fate or just bad luck.

"Can we call a truce long enough to talk about what happened years ago? And before you say no, think about how many times you've seen me this week and the disasters that followed. Do you really want to risk running into me again before I leave town?"

The left side of her mouth lifted, and it was as if someone had their hands wrapped around his neck, cutting off his air supply. With a spicy smile like that, she could probably get anything she wanted from him and any other man with a pulse.

He sighed in resignation. For years he'd wanted to

know why she'd left without telling him. He wanted—
no, needed—to hear what she had to say regarding her
departure back then, but was he ready?

"We were once very close. I don't want us to continue having this tension between us. Maybe you can
let me take you to dinner."

Austin shoved his hands into the front pockets of his
pants. It was time for him to deal with his issues with
Janna instead of allowing her betrayal to continue eating at him.

"I can't let you buy me dinner."

She shrugged. "Even better! You can treat me to dinner." Her lips twitched, trying to hide a grin.

Austin couldn't help but chuckle. Her bubbly personality, which he'd missed, was shining through. He'd
always been more serious than most, almost brooding,
where Janna had always been like a breath of fresh air
with a ready smile for anyone she came in contact with.

The office door swung open, catching their attention.
Nash stood in the doorway. Instead of walking into the
room, he just looked from one to the other.

"Is it safe to come in?"

"Funny," Janna said. "It's all good, especially since
Austin is insisting on taking me out to dinner."

Nash lifted an eyebrow at Austin before he walked
farther into the office. All Austin could do was shake
his head and shrug. The thought of spending time with
Janna, just the two of them, put him on edge. Not because he thought the discussion would get heated. No,
it had more to do with the lust coursing through his
veins. In the past, he'd had very little self-control when

it came to her. Even considering their situation, he knew it would be much the same.

"Well, since you have a dinner date, I suppose you want to postpone our meeting," Nash said to Janna.

"Why don't I wait outside while you two talk?" Austin headed to the door.

"You don't have to leave." Janna touched his shoulder, sending a bolt of electricity racing to the tips of his fingers. "I'd like for you to stay."

Nash folded his arms across his chest as they all stood near each other. "Actually, Janna, I'm not sure if you know this, but Austin is a financial guru. Since he's insisting on taking you out to dinner, maybe he can give you some suggestions on how best to deal with your situation."

Why does it feel like I've been set up?

"That would be great." Janna looked up at him with those beautiful doe eyes. How could she even think about getting his help, considering the way things stood between them?

Without giving him a chance to say yea or nay, she explained the situation regarding the financial management firm and one of their accountants.

Austin was wealthy and oversaw the finances for Reynolds Development, but he had no doubt that Janna's wealth exceeded anything he had ever managed.

"Though I'm sure Austin will have some recommendations, I'll give you the information for the accountant I use," Nash said and pulled the contact information up on his cell phone before jotting it down on the pad of paper on his desk.

Austin and Janna stared at each other, both lost in their own thoughts. He couldn't believe he was actually planning to help her. He couldn't help it. Despite whatever had prompted their relationship to fall apart and what he'd felt for her over the last couple of years, there was still nothing he wouldn't do to help her.

Nash cleared his throat. "Well, look at the time." He gathered his cell phone and his keys. "I need to pick up my boys, but if you guys want to hang out here longer, not a problem. Just let my manager know once you leave and he'll lock up the office."

"Actually, if it's okay with you," Austin said to Janna, "maybe we can head out, too."

"Sounds good." Janna lifted her large handbag. "I'm ready when you are."

A half an hour later, Austin escorted Janna into a popular restaurant in Midtown Atlanta. She was an attention magnet without trying. He would have preferred to cook dinner for her. At least if he'd taken her to his place, he wouldn't have to worry about pictures in newspapers. Then again, on his own turf, it would be just the two of them. And with the desire he'd seen in her eyes and the lust fluttering around in his gut, taking her home with him probably wouldn't have been the best idea.

Heads turned the moment they walked into the restaurant. Maybe it was because they were two unusually tall people, but then the murmurs started. They walked past a table with a group of guys and Austin moved closer to her and placed a hand at the small of her back. How she managed to deal with the attention without it fazing her was a mystery to him.

"Thank you," she said when he pulled out a chair for her and took the seat next to her. In light of the conversation they needed to have, he had requested that they be seated in the back of the restaurant. On the ride over, the initial tension between them had thawed, but Austin wasn't sure how their long overdue talk was going to go. He wanted to understand what had happened all those years ago in hopes of finding some closure. He just hoped he was ready for whatever she had to say.

"I don't know how you do it," Austin said after their server took their drink order.

"Do what?"

"I don't know how you deal with the stares everywhere you go. From the moment we walked through the door, you were the center of attention."

"How do you know they weren't looking at you?"

"Trust me, they were definitely not looking at me," he muttered and opened the menu.

Janna studied his handsome face. Austin was fine enough to be on the cover of any national magazine. With his sexy brown eyes, chiseled jaw and full, kissable lips, she'd bet her agent would sign him in a heartbeat if Austin showed an interest. But he hated attention. Always had. As one of the stars of their high school's basketball team, he'd blown off any accolades and always preferred to keep a low profile.

"Are you two ready to order? Maybe I can start you with an appetizer?" the server asked when she placed

Janna's white wine on the table as well as Austin's beer. She gave a quick rundown of their specials and then she really caught Janna's attention when she leaned over Austin's menu. While pointing out some of her favorite dishes, she brought attention to her large breasts in her low-cut shirt. Little did she know, Austin was a leg man. That knowledge still didn't keep jealousy from stirring inside of Janna. Sure she hadn't been with Austin in years, but witnessing some shameless hussy practically throwing herself at him made her see red… or green. She wanted to grab hold of the woman's long hair and give it a hard tug.

Austin closed his menu and looked at Janna. "I think I know what I want. What about you?"

Janna nodded, trying to ignore his choice of words. She was tempted to tell him exactly what she wanted, and it didn't include food. What she really wanted had more to do with his tempting lips, his muscular body and those large hands that used to touch her in all the right places.

She shook her head to free the wayward thought and quickly glanced down at the menu in her hands.

Okay. Focus, Janna, focus.

From the moment she'd stepped into Nash's office and seen him standing there, her body had been on high alert. She really did believe it was fate that they kept running into each other, though she had a feeling he thought she and Nash had set him up to be there when she arrived. Janna wasn't sure why her brother-in-law hadn't told her that he was meeting with someone else, but she was glad he hadn't.

Janna gave the server her order. Rarely did she eat soul food, but when Austin suggested the historic restaurant, she couldn't pass up the opportunity to try it out. Her first inclination was to order a salad, but she squashed the idea. She was on vacation. Instead, she ordered the restaurant's famous fried chicken and a side order of broccoli.

"And for you?" the server asked Austin, batting her fake eyelashes. Janna rolled her eyes and glanced away before she said something she would later regret.

"I'll have the catfish entrée and a glass of water."

"All right, I'll get that water out to you right away and your meals will be out shortly."

"So does that happen often?" Janna asked.

"What?"

"Servers who practically sit in your lap while trying to take your order."

Austin shook his head and laughed. "No. I can honestly say that doesn't often happen, probably because I rarely eat at restaurants. Normally I cook or order carryout."

He had always carried himself as if he were much older than his years. They were only a year apart in age, but in high school they were two years apart due to him skipping fifth grade. Cooking was one of his favorite pastimes. He used to prepare elaborate meals even as a teen. He had often told her that he liked cooking for her and had vowed to take care of her once they married.

Janna sipped from her glass of wine, wondering where to start in regard to their conversation. On the car ride over, small talk flowed between them, but neither had broached the topic that needed to be discussed.

"Why'd you leave me without a word or without saying goodbye? No note. No call. Nothing."

Well, so much for not knowing where to start, Janna thought. She sighed and set her wineglass down on the table, placing her hands in her lap. When she looked up at Austin, his face was expressionless, but his dark eyes bored into her.

"Austin…everything happened so quickly. I received a call from a modeling agency, offering the opportunity of a lifetime if I agreed to leave for Milan immediately. You and your family were on that two-week cruise to Hawaii and I couldn't reach you by telephone, which is why I sent you the letter."

He leaned forward. "What letter?"

A sense of dread crawled up Janna's back. "What do you mean, what letter? I wrote you the day I left, telling you what happened and that I would call you as soon as I could."

"Janna, I never received a letter or a telephone call."

"I swear to you that I mailed it on my way to the airport. I don't understand how you didn't get it. As for the phone call… I tried, but your number was disconnected and I later found out you and your family had moved."

"We didn't move to Atlanta until two months after you left."

"I… I." Janna glanced down and toyed with the black cloth napkin in her lap. She only had one shot to clear the air between them. Austin might've been one of the most patient people she knew, but he hated lies, or as she often referred to them, half truths. "When I didn't hear from you after sending you the letter, I assumed you didn't want anything to do with me. A few months went by before I swallowed my pride and decided to take my chances and call you."

Within seconds, his calm demeanor changed, his jaw clenched and his eyes narrowed. He gripped the side of the table as if trying to rein in his temper.

Before he could speak, the server returned to their table with their meals.

Janna's stomach churned with anxiety. She'd realized the conversation wouldn't be easy, but it was much harder than she had expected. She had never thought about the fact that he might not have received the letter. When she'd told her family that she hadn't heard from Austin, Mama Adel said that it was probably for the best and that she should focus on her career.

"Is there anything else I can get you?" the server asked, her gaze bouncing from Austin to Janna and back as if sensing the tension.

"No, everything is fine." Austin's clipped tone had the server hurrying away.

"I called you," Austin said. "As a matter of fact, I called you four times, to be exact."

Janna sat stunned.

"Once we returned from vacation, imagine my surprise when I went by your house and your mother said you were in Milan. Do you have any idea how that made me feel? To find out the girl I'd loved and planned to spend the rest of my life with had left the country without a word?"

Guilt lodged in Janna's throat. Her hand went to her chest, making small circles as if the move could release some of the tension that had built from the anguish she heard in his tone.

"Your mother gave me your manager's number, saying it was the only way to reach you. I called. The first two times, I left a message with him for you to call me back."

"Oh my God, Austin, I didn't know. He never told me."

"The last two times I left messages on his voice mail."

Janna was going to kill Nelson. How could he have not told her? He'd known how much Austin meant to her.

"Austin—" she reached out and placed her hand on top of his "—I'm so sorry. I didn't know. I would have called you back had I known." His gaze went to where her hand rested on top of his and he surprised her when he didn't pull away.

"Whether your manager gave you the messages or not, that's no excuse for you not calling me."

"I thought you were angry with me after receiving my letter. When I didn't hear from you, I just assumed…" Her words trailed off. There was nothing else she could say, and no other excuse she could give to explain her actions.

"How could you think that I wouldn't try calling? You knew how I felt about you." He turned his hand over and grasped her hand, squeezing a little as he continued. "I had planned to make you my wife. How could you think I wouldn't try to find you?"

Janna lowered her gaze and shook her head, fighting

the tears that pricked the back of her eyes. She should have known that Austin would try contacting her. Even at a young age, he was the most responsible, loyal person she'd ever known. He had always been clear about his feelings for her and wasn't shy about telling her how much he loved her. This…all of this was on her.

She looked up at him, her vision distorted by unshed tears. "I should have known." She lifted her napkin from her lap and dabbed at the corners of her eyes, trying hard not to let a tear fall. If one slipped through, more would follow. Thankfully, her back was to the majority of the other patrons.

"Listen, maybe talking about this out in public wasn't a good idea."

Janna shook her head. "No. I'm glad we're having this conversation. We should have had it years ago. I'm not happy with my manager, but ultimately, this whole mess is my fault."

Austin sighed and picked up his fork. "Why don't we eat while you tell me how everything played out?"

The last thing Janna wanted to do was eat, but she was glad he was willing to at least listen to her. Not that she was surprised. He'd had plenty of opportunities to practice patience and tolerance when it came to dealing with her. She hadn't been the most levelheaded person back in the day, especially considering the number of messes she used to get into. That often led to disagreements with Austin, but he never stayed mad long. He had once told her that his parents had a rule—never go to bed angry at each other. Austin had told her early on that he wanted that to be the case with them.

"The morning after you and your family left on vacation, I was contacted by Nelson, my current manager. On a whim, months earlier, I had sent him my head shots and a note expressing an interest in modeling."

"Why didn't you tell me you were querying modeling agencies? When we were making plans, you never mentioned modeling."

"I didn't mention it because I knew the chances of me becoming a model were slim. And besides, I was excited about the plans you had made for us." And she was. Austin was not only the most popular jock at their school, but he was also the smartest man she knew. He was valedictorian of his graduating class and everyone knew he had a promising future ahead of him.

Janna had known a life with him would be amazing and she couldn't wait to marry him. But thanks to lack of communication, she would never know what could have been.

She enjoyed the life she had built for herself, but a sadness swirled around inside her. What if she could have had both, her career and a life with Austin? This sweetheart of a man could have still been hers, had she handled things differently back then.

My plans. Therein lay the first problem, Austin thought. When he was making plans for their future, he had never realized that she saw them as *his* plans. Not their plans.

"What was in the letter?"

As far as he knew, she'd never lied to him. If she had sent the letter, as she claimed, what happened to it?

She set down her fork and wiped her mouth. It didn't go unnoticed that she had only taken one or two bites of her meal. If this was any indication how she normally ate, it was no wonder she was so thin.

"It stated that I loved you and that I hope you could understand that I had to go after this chance of a lifetime. I also mentioned that I wanted you to join me in Milan, maybe attend college there. I even offered to send you plane fare once I received my first check."

He would have appreciated the offer had he received it, but there was no way he would have taken money from her. He was old-school like his dad and didn't believe in letting a woman pay his way.

"I would have come," he said quietly. Hell, he probably would have stayed. He had been that in love with her.

"You would have?"

"Of course. Janna, you knew how I felt about you. I was serious about us having a life together, no matter where." He didn't like seeing the sadness in her eyes, which was so unlike her. Very little got Janna down, and he hated that their conversation had made the twinkle in her eyes disappear.

Her gaze returned to the plate in front of her. "I know," she said barely above a whisper. "Despite the way I left, the feelings were mutual. But later when I talked with my mother, she said I wasn't being fair to you. That you had a promising future and we were too young to be thinking about marriage."

His parents felt the same way, but Austin hadn't cared. He had always accomplished anything he'd set his mind to, and together they could have made it work. Yet he never got the chance. Janna took the option from him when she boarded the flight to Milan and didn't look back.

"I'll never be able to apologize to you enough for the hell I put us both through. I've missed you, Austin, and I never meant to hurt you. I was young…impulsive, and I thought… I honestly thought we could make it work. But when I didn't hear from you…" Her voice trailed off.

"Yeah, I know. I felt the same way. I'm sorry, too. I'm sorry I didn't try harder to get a hold of you." He took a swig of his beer, still a little amazed that he was sitting across from her in the flesh. "Back in Nash's office, you asked if we could call a truce."

"Can we?"

He nodded. The conversation with his father was at the front of Austin's mind. "Yeah. Let's try to put this behind us."

"I'd like that." She smiled for the first time since arriving at the restaurant and his heart constricted. Her smile had always sent a warm heat flowing through his body, and based on the last couple of hours, she still had the same effect on him. The attraction between them was more intense than ever, and that wasn't a good thing.

"So why don't you tell me more about this accountant of yours."

They talked and ate. It wasn't quite like old times, but it was as if a weight had been lifted off Austin. She was still animated when she talked, gesturing with her hands, her voice rising and falling as she explained her disappointment with the financial management company.

"There's something else I'd like to talk to you about."

"What's that?" Austin asked, the seriousness of her tone making him wonder if he really wanted to know.

"My nonprofit organization."

Now this surprised him. Janna had always been interested in fashion, makeup and other girly things, but he'd never known her to have any interest in philanthropy.

"I want to create a nonprofit to benefit children who are aging out of the foster care system. Many end up jobless and homeless once they turn eighteen. I have a plan that can keep some of these kids off the street. I was lucky, but so many don't end up in a loving home or with a family that looks out for them."

She told him more about her plans, and the more she talked, the more interested Austin became. Not just because he could tell the cause was close to her heart, but also because of the emotion in her voice. She'd always been a little quirky, easygoing and out to have a good time. Yet, he couldn't ever remember her speaking so seriously and passionately about a subject.

"I have a draft of my business plan back at my hotel if you'd like to see it." Her eyes held a vulnerability that he had never seen in her before. "I would really appreciate your opinion, and I'm open to any suggestions you have on how to proceed. I know your family has always been active in various causes."

Austin nodded. "Yeah, they still are, and I'd be glad to help you in any way that I can." His only concern was the idea of going back to her hotel room. He wasn't sure if he trusted himself not to do something crazy when they got there, like taste her sweet lips again or lure her to the closest bed.

Chapter 6

"Are you married?"

Austin sputtered, coughed and choked on his beer, surprised by the question, which seemed to come out of nowhere.

"Sorry about that. Didn't mean to catch you off guard," Janna said, amused the question would shake him up.

"No. No, it's fine." He set his glass down and quickly wiped his mouth. "And no, I'm not married, and I don't have any children," he supplied as if knowing that question would be next.

Janna almost said *good*, but held back. She knew it was too much to hope that they could pick up where they left off, but knowing he wasn't married was a start. Her feelings for him were just as strong as they once were and she'd give anything if they could at least be friends.

"I assume you're not married."

She quirked a smile and shook her head. Something that big would've been splashed across various magazines before she could finish saying *I do*. The media seemed to be able to capture everything about her. Well, almost everything. They still hadn't figured out her parentage and she prayed she could keep it that way.

"So did you two leave room for dessert?" the server asked as she collected Austin's empty plate.

"None for me," Janna said and requested a carryout container. Despite the food being good, most of her meal was still on her plate. She couldn't concentrate on eating. She wanted to focus on reestablishing a friendship with Austin. Yet sitting across from him, staring into his dark eyes, had her longing for more. It might be selfish, but she wanted what they once had.

"I'll pass, too. Can you bring us the check?"

"Sure, I'll be right back."

"I think I'll take this opportunity to run to the ladies' room." Austin discreetly pointed her in the right direction and stood, pulling out her chair. "I'll be right back."

A sudden tension circled around them. At first, she thought it was something she might have said or done. But after following his gaze to a table of men, she knew it was his protective nature kicking in. She had noticed the group when they walked in, making sure not to make eye contact, but felt their gazes on her.

Turning to Austin, she touched his arm. "Relax, I'll be fine." She headed to the restroom, an extra pep in her step. She didn't want to get too excited that maybe Austin still had feelings for her, but she couldn't help it. His protective claws wouldn't have come out if he didn't feel something. Or would they? On second thought, Austin had always been chivalrous, even at a young age.

Janna made quick work of using the bathroom and touching up her makeup. When she stepped out of the restroom, she startled. A man stood in the small area between the men's and women's bathrooms as if waiting on someone.

She nodded an acknowledgment, prepared to head back to her table, but he touched her arm.

Janna jerked away and took a step back. She could handle fans stopping to ask questions, but she didn't like people touching her without her permission.

"I'm sorry." He quickly lifted his hands as if surrendering. "I didn't mean to scare you, but aren't you Janna Morgan?"

She sighed. This was one evening she wished she could have gone without being noticed or approached.

"Yes, I am," she said and tried to step around him, but he blocked her way. She felt more irritated than threatened. "Will you excuse me, please?"

"Listen, I mean no harm, but I was wondering if I could get a picture with you."

Rarely did she roam around alone, especially considering how bold people were getting in their approach. She had recently seen a photo of herself with a male fan floating around on social media with a raunchy caption. It was then she knew she had to make some changes. One being she no longer took pictures with random men. Though she was comfortable with the decision, this was the first time she'd received the request since then. Now she debated how to handle the situation without things getting ugly.

Austin glanced toward the restroom area, getting a little concerned about Janna's delay. He was protective by nature, which was how he and Janna first met. He would never forget that day. She had shown up at the school's gym during one of his basketball practices in search of the gym teacher. Gorgeous even back then, she'd attracted some unwanted attention from one of his teammates. The gym teacher had left for the day, and his coach hadn't shown up yet, leaving the guys to practice unsupervised. One of the boys on the team suggestively offered to help her with whatever she needed. Even now, recalling how his teammate wouldn't back off when she told him she wasn't interested had Austin clenching his fist.

"Here you go, handsome. You can pay me whenever you're ready," the server said, interrupting his thoughts when she set the check on the table. "I hope to see you in again sometime…soon." Her wink and parting words weren't lost on Austin, especially since he had noticed her flirtatious attempts earlier. As he had earlier, he ignored her.

He glanced at the bill as his mind took him back to that time in the gym. Janna had been livid when he jumped in and punched his teammate, claiming she could take care of herself. That encounter led to him asking her out on a date. She would only agree if he promised not to punch every guy who spoke to her. Two years of dating resulted in two fights and one suspension from school. He could honestly say that if he had to do those times over, he'd do the exact same thing. He would fight for her.

Like you fought to keep her? He shook the annoying thought from his mind and stuffed enough cash in the black folder to cover the cost of their meal and a tip.

Austin grabbed her to-go container and headed in the direction of the restrooms, but stopped short. One of the men from the rowdy table was blocking Janna's path.

His pulse ratcheted up and a wave of annoyance coursed through his body. Like years ago, his first thought was to swing first and ask questions later, but he was older, wiser. Or so he told himself.

Don't do anything stupid. The last thing you want is to end up on social media or in another article.

Janna looked up, and her eyes grew big when she spotted him. No doubt she thought he might make a scene.

"Hey, sweetheart." The endearment flowed out of his mouth as if it were the most natural thing to say. "What's going on?"

"Hey, man, I don't mean any harm. I was just asking to get a photo with her. You know how it is," the guy said as if he had a right to take a picture with Janna.

"No, actually, I don't. But I do know that outside her job, I'm the only man who takes pictures with her." He moved past the man and extended his hand to Janna. "Ready to go?"

At first taken aback, her mouth hanging open, she quickly recovered.

A slow smile lifted the left corner of her lips. "As a matter of fact, I am." She grabbed hold of his hand and winked at him, sending a wave of lust shooting through his body. "I was on my way back to the table."

Might as well keep the show going.

Once her hand rested in his larger one, he lifted it to his lips, placing a slow kiss on the inside of her wrist. She shivered and her eyes stared into his.

"Let's get out of here." He pulled her close and she molded to him without missing a beat, her arm going around his waist.

"Sounds good." They started walking away, but she stopped and turned back to her admirer. "Have a good evening."

Neither of them spoke as they walked through the establishment. Austin relished having her close. She fit so perfectly against his body, as if she were made specifically for him.

When they stepped outside and he handed the valet ticket to the attendant, Austin didn't release her right away.

"Thank you for what you did back there." Janna looked up at him. His eyes immediately zoned in on her lips and it was taking every bit of restraint he had not to lower his head and cover her mouth with his.

"You're welcome. So does *that* happen often?" he asked, using her words from earlier.

She offered a slight smile and pulled slightly away from him. "Sometimes. Most times when I'm out and about, I'm usually with a friend, my manager or one of my sisters. So guys aren't as bold in those instances. But normally the situations are harmless."

As far as Austin was concerned, that particular situation hadn't seemed harmless. It burned him up inside to see guys fawning over her. He hated thinking that he was the jealous type, but when it came to Janna, he wasn't himself.

He lowered his hand to the small of her back when the attendant pulled up in his Porsche. Austin helped her into the vehicle before handing the valet a generous tip and climbing into the driver's side of the car.

"Where are you staying?"

"The Marriott Marquis downtown," Janna said and fastened her seat belt. "Thank you for dinner. Nice place, and the food was good."

He glanced at her with raised eyebrows. "How would you know? You barely ate."

Janna chuckled. "Well, what I ate was good and the wine was excellent. Besides, tonight was all about the company. Spending the evening with you was like old times."

Austin nodded, his attention on the road. "I agree. I forgot how comfortable you always made me feel. This was nice."

"I never really apologized for the photo that ended up in the entertainment section the other day," Janna said, turning her body slightly despite the restraint of the seat belt. "I didn't mean to bring any negative attention on you."

He gave a half shrug. "It's all right. I'll admit I was

livid when I first saw it." Funny what a difference a couple of days made. He'd never expected to spend time with her ever again.

"I'm sure. I know how you hate attention. Well, I assume that's still the case."

"It is," he said. That was a major difference between them. Janna had always loved people and enjoyed being a part of the in crowd, whereas he preferred to be alone if he wasn't with her.

"I noticed you're in the media often."

"Not by choice. Well, at first it was because my manager said that I needed to stay visible. For the last year or so, I've tried to be mindful about who I'm seen with, especially when I started working on my nonprofit. I want people to see me as more than the model who graces the covers of national magazines. I want to be taken seriously, so I've been working on cleaning up my image."

"So the photo from the other day, did it help or hurt the image you're trying to portray?"

She thought for a moment before speaking. Another sign of her maturing. Gone was the girl who spoke first and thought later. He could remember plenty of times when she'd had to dig herself out of situations her mouth got her into.

Austin was suddenly looking forward to getting to know this older version of Janna Morgan.

"Considering how well respected you are, the photo might have helped my image. I'm embarrassed to say that it probably didn't hurt it. The media is good at twisting situations, making it seem as if I'm romantically involved with every man I'm seen with. And it's far from the truth," she hurried to add. She didn't know why it was so important to her that Austin knew that she wasn't the person the media made her out to be. Yes, she liked to have a good time, but she didn't sleep around. Besides Austin, she had only been in one other serious relationship. And even then, it couldn't compare with what she shared with him.

"Well, I'm glad I could help, though I had to take some serious ribbing from my brother. A couple of guys I play ball with insisted that I'd been holding out on them or I'd photoshopped you into the picture."

Janna laughed. "How is Malcolm? I saw him before I left the fundraiser, but I didn't get a chance to speak to him."

"He's all right. He's still a pain in the you-know-what, but I've kept him around this long. I feel like I'm stuck with him."

Janna always did love the brothers' bond. Austin and his brother were only a couple of years apart and were as different as night and day. Where Austin preferred quiet and was very studious, Malcolm was a partier. He'd been in college when she and Austin dated, but he always returned home on the weekends. When he wasn't harassing Austin, he was entertaining some girl or attending a party.

"So tell me about yourself. I know you're the CFO of your family's company, but what do you do for fun?"

He laughed and was slow to respond.

Janna wouldn't be surprised if he was still a work-aholic. During his senior year in high school, he held down two part-time jobs. Whenever he wasn't at school or with her, he was working. His plan was to pay his own way through college. Even when several scholarships came through, he continued to work, claiming that he wanted to make sure he had enough money saved up for their future.

Another jolt of guilt lodged in her gut. She shouldn't have left him. It didn't matter that they had probably been too young back then to be discussing marriage and having a family; she wanted what he wanted. She had been looking forward to being Mrs. Austin Reynolds.

In hindsight, she wished she would have waited and talked to Austin instead of just leaving. If the modeling agency had really been interested in her, they would have understood her needing a couple of weeks before flying to Milan. She knew that now. At that time, she had no clue to how the modeling world worked.

"Well, as you probably guessed, I work a lot," Austin said pulling her back to the present. "When I'm not working, I'm traveling for work. And during those rare occasions that I have free time, I play ball and do some woodworking."

A smile tilted the corner of her lips. "So you still play with wood, huh?" They laughed. "I still have the jewelry box you gave me for my fifteenth birthday."

"Really?"

"Of course. To this day it's one of the best gifts I've ever received."

"In that case, you need to start hanging out with some better gift givers. Oh, and I see you still have the ring."

She held her right hand out in front of her, gazing at

the ring he'd given her, one of many gifts over a two-year dating period. Despite the way her young life had started, Austin had given her some wonderful memories.

"I never leave home without it. The only time I take it off is if I'm doing a photo shoot. Other than that, I wear it wherever I go."

"Why?"

She glanced at him, caught off guard by the question. She stared at him for a moment before returning her attention to the ring.

"It makes me feel as if you're with me. Going to Milan at sixteen by myself was the scariest thing I'd ever done. I think I cried every day for the first month. So many times, I considered returning home. Returning to you. Even when I finally admitted that things were over between us, I couldn't part with it. I lost you, but somehow wearing your ring made it not hurt as much."

Austin didn't speak. Instead, he reached over and held her hand. This was a good sign. Maybe they could be friends…if not more. Guilt had been her companion for years for choosing her career over the person she had planned to spend the rest of her life with.

They continued talking and Austin told her how his parents had relocated them to Atlanta a month before he started at Morehouse. Hearing him talk about his college life and the glimpses of what he'd been up to after graduating made her wonder how different her life would have been had she chosen him over her career.

She turned to the passenger side window and watched the city pass in a blur. For years, she'd assumed that he had ignored her letter, not bothering to contact her. The thought that this could have been cleared up many years earlier made her mad at herself…and angry at Nelson. And there was a part of her that was a little disappointed in Austin. He should have tried harder to get in contact with her. Then again, at this moment, none of it mattered.

Once they arrived at the hotel, they took the elevator up to her penthouse suite. Janna couldn't ever recall being this nervous around a man, especially Austin. During the ride to the hotel, they'd talked and laughed like old friends. Though her feelings for him were as intense as ever, she didn't expect him to forgive and forget. It was a good sign that he was talking to her, willing to teach her the basics of managing her finances and look over her business plan.

They stood outside her hotel room and Janna wondered how she'd handle being in such close quarters with him. Even now, he hovered behind her as she fumbled with the key card, his warmth doing wicked things to her. She was tempted to lean back into his arms and soak up the heat radiating off him, making her even more nervous about going inside.

"Come in," she said when she finally pushed the door open. "Make yourself comfortable."

The one-bedroom king-size suite was beautifully decorated with a gold-and-brown color palette, accented with big, comfortable furniture.

Janna set her handbag and the key card on the table near the door. Austin took a slow glance around, then walked over to the wall-to-wall windows that gave a magnificent view of downtown Atlanta.

"I'll be right back. I'm going to grab the business plan."

"Okay," he said, his gaze still on what was beyond the windows.

She hurried into the bedroom, kicked off her high heels and stepped into a pair of flip-flops. After a quick glance in the mirror to check her makeup, she pulled her hair into a ponytail. Now comfortable, she returned to the living room with the binder that had become like a companion.

Austin turned and gave her a once-over. His appreciative gaze finally made it back to her face. Was he like her, feeling that this time together was surreal? Janna handed him the binder. "Can I get you something to drink?"

"How about water?" He made his way to the sofa and opened the binder.

"Coming right up."

"Did you do all of this yourself?" he asked when she handed him the bottled water and sat next to him.

"Yes."

The heat that propelled through her when their legs touched was almost her undoing, their attraction much more intense than she remembered. It was as if she was fighting against an invisible force. She was trying to keep her distance. Yet there was a pull between them that made her want to move closer. Much closer. It wasn't just the scent of his cologne that drew her; it was everything about him. Gorgeous without even knowing it, Austin was the type of man who drew women's attention. There was such a presence about him. Tall with a muscular build, he was not only *fine*, but highly intelligent. She'd always been attracted to intellectual men.

"Yes, I used business planning software," she finally responded to his question. "I've been working on this project for over a year."

"It shows. It's very detailed and it looks as if you've covered everything that an investor would ask about. Impressive."

She couldn't stop a smile from spreading across her mouth. Coming from him, that was high praise. It seemed as though the decision to continue her education was paying off.

Janna had left for Milan before graduating from high school, but obtained her GED. She had always wanted to return to school and recently started an online program to obtain her bachelor's degree. Instead of majoring in fashion design the way she'd planned to do after graduating from high school, she'd enrolled in an accelerated business program. Despite her success as a model, she had always felt inferior to her sisters—one being a doctor, the other a lawyer—and needed to prove to herself, if no one else, that she could obtain her degree.

"Since you said that you would give me some pointers on how to oversee my finances, do you think you can help me with the budget for this project?" She was prepared to use any excuse to spend more time with him, but she really did want to hear what he thought about the financials.

"How long are you in town for?"

"I'll be here for two more weeks before heading back to New York." Just the thought of leaving him when they were getting reacquainted left an emptiness in the pit of her stomach.

"What does your schedule look like?"

"I'm on vacation. Since you're willing to help me, I'll be more than happy to work around your schedule."

He closed the binder and set it on the table in front of the sofa before standing. "If you're free tomorrow evening, maybe we can have dinner, then spend some time on the budget, as well as discuss your accounting situation."

Excitement rippled inside Janna, but she tried not to let it show. She so wanted to get to know him again and would do almost anything to make it happen.

"I'd like that." They exchanged contact information and she walked with him to the door.

"I'll give you a call in the morning with the details about dinner," he said, his hand on the doorknob.

Instead of opening the door, he turned and their gazes collided. Janna's heart stuttered when his dark stare bored into her and the desire she saw in his eyes matched what she felt deep in her soul. She didn't know who moved first, but without saying a word, their lips touched. All she could think about was how much she wanted this. Needed this.

His tongue nudged her lips apart and his arms eased around her waist, pulling her gently against him. He deepened the kiss and electric jolts shot to every nerve ending in her body. His kiss was slow and thorough. Janna melted into him. Her hands glided up his rock-hard chest and one went easily to the back of his head, pulling him closer, hungry for more of what he was offering.

Flattened against him, she felt the proof of his desire rubbed up against her stomach, sending a sweet thrill through her body. Her heart pounded harder. She wanted nothing more than to throw caution to the wind and ask him to stay.

All too quickly, Austin ended the kiss but was slow to pull away. They stood, staring at each other, lost in the strong connection they shared. He caressed her cheek with the back of his fingers before completely releasing her.

"I'll see you tomorrow. Have a good night."

Janna continued staring at the closed door long after Austin's departure, her lips still warm from his kiss. He had never been shy about what he wanted, and apparently that hadn't changed. But what did it mean? Her feelings for him were as strong as they'd been years ago, but she had no idea how he felt about her. If the passion she witnessed in his eyes and the kiss he had planted on her were any indication, it was mutual.

She moved across the room, still shaken, and dug through her handbag for her cell phone. There was something she needed to take care of and she needed to do it sooner than later.

She speed-dialed the person who could have impacted her life in a different way years ago.

"Hi, doll. I'm surprised to hear from you, since you're on vacation."

"How could you, Nelson?"

Silence. "How could I what?"

"How could you have not told me that Austin Reynolds called me more than once when you first signed me?"

He hesitated again. "I did that for your own good. You were young and had one shot to make it big. I didn't want you distracted."

"That wasn't up to you, Nelson!"

"Well, technically it was. Janna, you were a minor and you were my responsibility. I did what I thought was best for you."

Anger singed every cell in her body and it was probably good they weren't face-to-face.

"You knew how I felt about him. He was the most important person in my life and you knew that. I can't believe you did that to me." Had she heard from Austin, she wasn't sure what would've happened, but Nelson had taken the decision out of her hands.

Hurt and rage coiled inside her. She struggled not to say something that she might regret later. Then again, he deserved any tongue-lashing she gave him. Because of him, she had missed the most valuable years of her life with the only man she had ever loved.

"Just so that we're clear, Nelson, you don't get to decide who I talk to or who I don't. I want all of my messages and then I'll decide whether or not I'll call someone back."

"Doll, you should be thanking me for all that I've done for you and for your career. You're wealthy and one of the most sought-after models in the industry because of me."

Janna paced the length of the living room, breathing hard and struggling to keep her anger at bay.

"You know what, Nelson? I appreciate all that you have done for me over the years, but let's not forget what I've done for *your* career. You are wealthy because of me. None of your other clients have brought you as much business as I have. So don't get it twisted."

Silence fell between them and Janna was tempted to hang up, knowing that Nelson was slow to ever admit any wrongdoing. She wondered what else he had taken upon himself to do as it related to her. This was a good example of why she needed to get better control of her life.

"You're right," Nelson finally said. "I had no right to withhold calls or messages from you. It won't happen again."

"You're right. It won't. You're fired!"

Chapter 7

Austin started his car and blasted the air conditioner. Only May, and already the temperature was in the mid-eighties.

What a day. A day full of meetings, crunching numbers and thoughts of Janna. He was doomed if a simple kiss could distract him from his everyday life. The night before, he had only planned to kiss her on the cheek and bid her good-night, but their gazes collided. It was as if his brain had short-circuited. All he could think about was having her in his arms and tasting her again. The desire he saw brimming in her beautiful eyes got the best of him and without warning, his body overruled his brain and his mouth covered hers.

He shook his head and drove toward her hotel. "What the heck am I doing? She's my past," he said aloud. He couldn't understand it. So many years had passed since he had last been with her, and after only a few hours, it was as if no time had elapsed. He still didn't know if she had really tried reaching out to him after leaving for Milan, but he wanted to believe her. *God, I want to believe her.* Unfortunately, there was still that little twinge of doubt lodged in the back of his mind. For so many years, he'd believed that she had given up on him, on them, to pursue her career.

I can't let her back into my life. No matter how strong the attraction between them, they couldn't go back to what they once had. She had almost broken his spirit when she walked out on him to pursue a modeling career. If he let himself fall for her again, who was to say that she wouldn't do the same thing? He wouldn't be able to recover from something like that again.

He pulled up to the front of the hotel and parked. Before he could exit the car, he saw her through the glass doors, sashaying toward him. His breath hitched when his gaze took in her denim short shorts and went lower. *Those legs.* His body rumbled to attention with thoughts of having those long, shapely legs wrapped around him. The self-talk on the ride over flew right out the window at the sight of her.

He swallowed hard but snapped to attention when a man she passed whistled at her. The guy's friend made a comment to her just as Austin stepped out of the car to open her door. He narrowed his eyes at the small group when Janna drew closer.

"Oh. My bad, man," the guy who whistled said. "I didn't mean any disrespect."

"Hi," Janna said, snatching Austin's full attention when she stepped to him and ran her hand up his arm seductively. Then she surprised the hell out of him. When she placed a lingering kiss on his lips, all thoughts of gawkers were pushed to the back of his mind. "It's good to see you."

He cleared his throat. "Uh, yeah. You, too." He opened the car door and helped her in.

"Lucky bastard," one of Janna's admirers grumbled before heading into the hotel.

Austin had a feeling Janna's actions were intended to get a rise out of the men watching. It worked. Hell, it also got a rise out of him.

He released a frustrated breath as he tried to get his body under control while strolling toward the driver's side. He felt like an adolescent crushing on the lead cheerleader, his body having a mind of its own.

He glanced over the roof of the car, where onlookers continued to watch. Any other time, he would have hated the attention they drew, but for some unexplainable reason, he was glad they had witnessed the interaction.

He climbed into the car and was immediately assaulted by Janna's seductive scent, which was potent enough to bring a man to his knees. Austin's gaze dropped to her smooth, crossed legs, and suddenly the decision to cook dinner for her at his place didn't seem like such a good idea. How the hell was he going to keep his hands off her? He groaned inside when he noticed her beach bag, probably holding the swimsuit he'd suggested she bring in order to take advantage of his pool.

I'm so screwed.

"How was work?" Janna asked, pulling him out of his thoughts. When he looked at her closely, he noticed for the first time since she walked out of the hotel that she didn't have that usual sparkle in her eye.

"It was all right," he said slowly. "What about you? How did your day go? Is everything okay?"

She nodded, her silence speaking volumes.

"You sure?" He slowed at a stoplight, giving her his full attention, noticing that her usual smile seemed forced.

"Yes. Everything's fine." She glanced away, which was when he really knew something was wrong.

Instead of pressuring her for details, he continued driving in silence until she spoke.

"I talked to my manager, Nelson, last night," she choked out. A quick glance in her direction showed no tears, but the emotion in her voice made Austin wonder if it weren't just a matter of time. He had only seen her cry two other times—once when she sprained her ankle playing volleyball, and once when her birth mother, whom Janna wanted nothing to do with, called her on her fifteenth birthday.

"I fired him."

"What?" Austin tightened his grip on the steering wheel. He slowed when the traffic suddenly started moving at a crawl. Normally he didn't leave work until seven in the evening in order to avoid rush hour. Today he'd made an exception. "Janna, I didn't tell you about the calls for you to fire him."

"I had to. He ruined a portion of my life. Granted, it

was my decision to go to Milan, but if I had known you called, we would have been together. I wouldn't have spent these years feeling guilty or being disappointed because I thought you didn't want me."

He definitely wanted her. Heck, he ached for her.

She rubbed her bare legs, drawing his attention to the way her hand moved slowly up and down her smooth skin. He wished it was him she was touching.

He reached for her hand to stop the movement, knowing it was the only way to regain his focus. He diverted his gaze back to the road. The traffic still hadn't moved. Her hand shook within his and he held it tighter.

"Baby, I'm sorry about everything. But it wasn't his fault. I shouldn't have given up. I could have…should have tried harder. I was young and my ego took a big hit when you left, but I shouldn't have given up until I heard from you. Until I heard you say with your own mouth that you didn't want to be with me."

"I never would have said that to you. I know the way I left gave you doubt, but I swear I never stopped loving you. If I could do things differently, I would. I have missed you…" Her voice trailed off and she quickly turned her attention to the passenger side window as if she'd said too much. It went without saying that Austin had missed her, too, but he didn't want her to jeopardize her career by acting too hastily regarding her manager.

"Janna, we were so young. What we had happened a long time ago."

She turned sad eyes to him. "That doesn't lessen what I felt for you. What I'll always feel for you."

Austin loosened his grip on her hand. The traffic

started moving again and he used that reason to release her as the silence inside the car grew heavy. Her admission caught him off guard. Was it possible that their feelings for each other could have really stood the test of time? She still held a special spot in his heart, but he couldn't let himself believe that she felt the same way.

"Nelson has managed my career…my life for almost ten years. Who knows what else he has done that might not have been in my best interest?"

Austin hated seeing her like this. He wanted the happy-go-lucky girl he once knew to show herself.

"I also talked to Mama Adel last night," she continued without prompting. "I asked her why she never told me that she'd given you Nelson's telephone number. I would have been happy to know she'd given you the number. All of these years, and I can't believe she never told me. Until yesterday, I had no idea you tried reaching me. They both knew how hard it was for me to stay in Milan with you being in the States."

He understood her pain. He knew about the ache in her heart that she probably thought would never heal. He knew about the constant questions running through her mind as she experienced sleepless nights thinking about him. And he knew the feeling of hopelessness that had followed for months after they parted ways. He prayed she hadn't felt the same pain that he'd experienced. He wouldn't wish that time in his life on his worst enemy.

"My mother said that we were too young to be talking about marriage. She said that when I told her that I hadn't heard from you, she thought it was for the best. We both had great opportunities, me with the modeling and you with several scholarships. We needed to pursue our own individual dreams, according to her."

He exited the highway, trying to shake the melancholy that suddenly filled the space. He turned up the air conditioner and gave himself a mental shake to clear his mind of memories he wanted to forget.

They arrived at Austin's home and he pulled into the long driveway. Anger rattled inside of him. Back then, everyone thought they knew what was best for him and Janna. Sure, they'd been young, but Austin had known what he wanted, and it was to spend the rest of his life with Janna.

"Your home is incredible." Janna quickly wiped her face with the back of her hand. He'd been so busy trying to rein in his anger, he hadn't noticed the tears or her red eyes.

"Thanks." He pulled into the three-car garage and lowered the automatic door, trying to figure out what to say to her.

Instead, he shut the engine off, unhooked both of their seat belts and pulled her into his arms. Holding her close, he placed a kiss against her temple and just held her. He'd missed having her in his arms.

They sat silent for a few minutes and he kissed her again before releasing her.

"I'm sorry…for everything. I have ruined our lives, and now I'm ruining our evening," she mumbled against his chest.

"Stop. Baby, just stop." He rubbed the back of her neck. "All of that was in the past. Let's agree to leave the past in the past for good. No more talks about what could or should've been. No more talks about who's to blame. Agreed?"

She nodded and took a deep breath, releasing it slowly. "We leave the past in the past."

Austin felt her tension ease as she glanced around his oversize garage.

"So are you going to feed me, or are you going to make me sit out here in this ridiculously clean garage?" Her beautiful smile returned and he laughed.

He released an exaggerated sigh. "Oh, all right. I guess I can feed you. Come on."

Janna had known his house would be gorgeous, but this exceeded her expectations. She stood in the middle of the wall-to-wall hardwood floors where she could see the huge kitchen, the family room and the formal dining room. She had often considered buying a single-family home instead of her Manhattan penthouse, but thought it would be too much for one person.

"Do you live alone?"

"Yes," he said after a short hesitation. She wondered what that was all about but didn't ask.

She set her bag in a comfortable-looking chair in the family room and strolled around the first floor, taking in the top-of-the-line fixtures and expensive furniture. By the looks of things, Austin had done very well for himself. Not that she was surprised. Anyone who knew him knew he would be a success.

"Make yourself at home. I'm going upstairs to change."

"Okay," she said absently as she made her way to the

mantel, where several framed photos were. She smiled at what appeared to be a recent picture of his family. Her gaze moved along to several others but stopped when she got to the one of Austin with a very pretty lady. Considering how close the two stood, their arms wrapped around each other, it was safe to say this was someone special to him. She lifted the frame. If their pose and smiles hadn't given it away, the way the woman stared up at Austin said it all. Janna recognized the look. She had worn it plenty of times when she and Austin were together.

She set the photo back down but didn't immediately walk away. There was still so much she didn't know about him. One thing she did know, though, was that he wouldn't have invited her over for dinner and a swim if he was involved with someone else.

Janna finished her tour of the first floor and then stepped out onto his impressive back deck. The covered outdoor kitchen would be a griller's dream space and she wondered if Austin entertained out there much. Everything, from the appliances to the cozy sitting area and table for eight, appeared brand-new. He had always been a neat freak and apparently that trait included his backyard space.

Gorgeous and *private* were her first thoughts as she perused the yard that was hidden from others by tall cedar trees. She leaned against the railing and took in the in-ground lap pool surrounded by lounge chairs. The numerous flower beds, strategically placed, had to be the source of the scent of roses that had permeated the air the moment she stepped outside.

"Did you want to eat first or go for a swim?" Austin said, stepping out onto the deck. Janna turned and an intense quiver raked over her flesh when he stood before her, all tall and sexy. The light blue T-shirt he wore stretched across his chest and showed off his thick biceps. Her pulse kicked up when her gaze went to his flat abs and the denim shorts that hung low on his hips. She loved that he opted for boat shoes versus sandals or flip-flops, which she hated seeing men wear.

"You look *good*," she said before she could catch herself. "I mean…I'm starving." *And not for food* was what she wanted to add, but she kept her mouth closed, letting him think whatever he wanted to think.

The corners of his lips lifted into a grin. "Then I guess I should feed you." His voice was seductively deep and by the desire in his eyes, Janna was reminded that they weren't kids anymore.

He extended his hand to her and she took it, wondering where he was leading her.

"Come on. You can help me cook."

Okay, that wasn't what she had in mind. "Just so you know, I still can't cook."

Austin shook his head and laughed. "Why am I not surprised?"

"In my defense, I travel more than I'm at home. So I haven't had much opportunity to learn."

"Mmm-hmm," he said, rinsing his hands in the kitchen sink. "If I'm not mistaken, you never had a desire to learn how."

"I'll admit, you're right. Maybe one of these days."

They laughed and talked as he instructed her on seasoning the chicken while he prepared the burgers. When he called earlier to ask her how she felt about them grilling outside, she had told him that she would give anything for a good, juicy burger. That was something she hadn't had in almost a year.

"I never got a chance to congratulate you on winning the bid Saturday night. I spoke to T'Keyah this afternoon."

Austin had earned huge points with Janna when she found out that he had bidden on the item she donated to the silent auction. Then he gave the gift to the daughter of a friend.

"T'Keyah was the first person I thought of when I saw what you were offering. She has had a tough time coping with her mother's death and I thought spending time with you would be just what she needed."

"I see you're still a sweetheart," Janna said, popping a grape into her mouth. Austin had pulled a fruit tray out of the refrigerator.

"I don't know about all of that. I'm sure others who bid had someone special in mind, too."

"Maybe." Janna pushed the tray of fruit away before she filled up on grapes and cantaloupe.

"So when are you meeting with her and what do you have planned?"

Janna explained to him her desire to help young women learn the proper techniques of applying makeup. She had also arranged with Nordstrom to bring T'Keyah for a mini shopping spree. That all would take place on Friday and then Saturday morning Janna would take her to a famous hairstylist. She wanted T'Keyah to look perfect for her prom Saturday night.

Once the food was done, Janna and Austin sat on the deck, reminiscing about their high school days. She was surprised to hear how many people they knew who had moved to Atlanta from Edison. Leaving school a year early, she hadn't kept in touch with anyone. Something she regretted.

An hour later, Janna and Austin were still on the deck talking. The setting sun helped bring the temperature down but it was still fairly warm outside.

"Why don't you take a dip in the pool while I clean up?" Austin suggested and stood with their plates. At that moment, lights around the pool flickered on.

"Are you sure you don't want me to help?"

"No, I have it. Oh, and there are towels in the cabinet to the right inside the cabana." He nodded toward the structure on the other side of the pool before disappearing into the house.

Janna stood and quickly undressed, her swimsuit beneath her clothes. She'd been eyeing the water all evening and couldn't wait to dive in. After a few laps, she hung against the edge of the pool, her body still submerged. She could get used to this. Normally her days were filled with traveling, photo shoots and attending various events. Rarely did she have a chance to just hang out and be carefree.

"I have a surprise for you," Austin said from behind her. She turned to find a bowl with two spoons hanging out. "Do you still love ice cream?"

"Are you kidding? Of course I do." She climbed out

of the pool, not missing his appreciative perusal of her white bikini. She should've felt bad about deciding to wear it for him, but she didn't. She wanted him to notice, and by the ardent look in his eyes, she received the results she was going for.

She took a slow stroll to the cabinet holding the towels, making sure to put a little something extra in her walk. She almost smiled when he cleared his throat before claiming one of the lawn chairs.

"So what type is it?" she asked when she sat next to him.

"Butter pecan, of course."

A smile covered her lips. "I can't believe you remembered."

"I remember everything about you," he said and held a spoonful of ice cream toward her.

Meeting his gaze, she opened her mouth and let him feed her. Eating ice cream and watching movies used to be their favorite pastime. *God, I've missed him.*

He continued feeding her, and the romantic gesture was turning her on. No other man had ever fed her, and even if one had, somehow she knew it wouldn't have been the same.

Some ice cream missed her mouth, falling to her chin. She lifted her hand to wipe it off, but he stopped her.

"Let me."

Instead of using the spoon, he lowered his head and his mouth touched her chin, his tongue tickling her. Heat shot through Janna's body and the erotic gesture sent warmth up her spine. It took everything within her to sit still and let him clean her up.

She swallowed hard when he lifted his head slightly, his eyes meeting hers. Without him saying a word, his lips met hers in the sweetest kiss. She whimpered when he captured her top lip and then her lower as he teased her with his gentleness. Oh, yeah, she could definitely get used to this.

He moved to her cheek and worked his way down her neck. When he made contact with the sensitive area behind her ear, she squirmed and giggled.

"I see you're still ticklish," he mumbled against her neck, nipping and licking. She fidgeted and couldn't take it anymore.

"Okay, okay." She laughed outright, trying to pull away from him. He had a loose grip on her and she leaped from the chair.

"Come back here. I'm not done with you yet. I think some ice cream dripped onto your shoulder."

She laughed. "I don't think so, Mr. Reynolds." She jumped into the pool, surprised when he jumped in after her, shoes and all. They laughed and played in the water. She loved seeing this fun, lighter side of him. So often growing up, he'd acted as if he carried the weight of the world on his shoulders, more serious than he needed to be. She remembered his mother saying that he had always been very serious, even as a child.

He chased her in the pool, making her laugh harder. When he caught up to her, he locked her in place, his arms on each side of her. "That's better." And his mouth covered hers again.

One of his arms went around her waist and her body molded to his. Janna looped her arms around his neck. She loved the feel of his hard body against hers. The evidence of his desire pressed against her stomach. Her heart thumped harder. His large hand covered her breasts, kneading and squeezing. His nimble fingers tweaked her nipple, eliciting a soft moan from her. Janna didn't know how much she could take. Her body was on fire.

Holding on to his neck tighter, she wrapped her legs around his waist. Now he was the one moaning as he ground against her. One of his arms held her securely around her waist as the other gripped the back of her head, deepening the kiss.

Moments later, his mouth pulled away, letting her come up for air. "God, I want you." His husky voice turned her on even more.

Before she could respond, he angled his head and captured her lips again, devouring her mouth. She arched into him when he lowered her slightly. Rotating her hips, she loved the feel of his erection grinding against her throbbing sex. The material between them had to go. She wanted to feel him. All of him.

"So, what do we have here?"

Austin dropped her legs and leaped back like a child caught with his hand in the cookie jar. They both turned in the direction of a woman's voice. Janna gave her a once-over, admiring the cute strapless dress with the matching sandals. Though she had no clue who the woman was, she immediately recognized her from the photo on the mantel.

Janna's gaze bounced from her to Austin as he cursed

under his breath, a pained expression darkening his features.

Yes, indeed. What do we have here?

Shocked to see Zoe standing on the side of the pool, Austin was temporarily at a loss for words. A quick glance at Janna, her eyebrows raised heavenward, and he knew he had some explaining to do, but first he had to get his body under control before climbing out of the pool. He'd gone from zero to fifty on the lust-for-Janna scale.

"Hey, Zoe. I wasn't expecting you."

"Apparently," she said, and Austin noticed a little attitude behind the one word.

"Janna, this is Zoe Davis. Zoe, Janna Morgan."

"I thought I recognized you," Zoe said to Janna. "But I'm a little surprised to see you kissing my…" Her voice trailed off and Austin felt more than saw Janna stiffen next to him.

"Your what?" Janna asked carefully.

Zoe hesitated, her gaze holding Austin's. "My… friend."

Austin released the breath he hadn't realized he was holding. Janna knew nothing about his engagement— that is, his broken engagement. Considering how they were getting along and how he felt about her, it was probably a conversation he should have had sooner rather than later.

"Austin, may I speak to you inside for a moment?" Zoe nodded toward the house. "Nice meeting you, Janna," she said before turning and walking away.

"Sorry about this," Austin whispered to Janna. "I'll explain everything in a minute."

"I'll be waiting."

Austin snatched a towel from the cabinet and hurried toward the house, tempted to look back when he heard Janna climb out of the water. He had to be the lowest form of human life, wanting to get another look at her skimpy bikini while another woman waited for him inside his house.

"Well, I guess I no longer have to wonder about the woman who holds your heart," Zoe said the moment he stepped into the kitchen. "It seems I missed a lot this week. Care to catch me up with what's been going on?"

Considering he was a man who didn't like drama and pretty much led a boring life, the past week had been anything but that.

"You deserve an explanation," he finally said. Then again, she was his *ex*. He really didn't have to explain anything to her, but he would. They were friends long before they got engaged and he had too much respect for her not to answer any questions she might have regarding Janna.

"Give me five minutes to get out of these wet clothes and I'll explain everything."

A short while later, he sat on the bar stool next to Zoe.

"Why don't you start with the photo I saw of the two of you earlier this week?"

Austin almost chuckled. Had it only been a week since he first ran into Janna? Or should he say, since *she* ran into him?

He told Zoe about the past week, including seeing Janna at the bakery as well as the fundraiser. Saying everything out loud, Austin was taken aback by how easy it had been for him and Janna to pick up where they left off, despite the way they had parted ways. Had someone told him a month ago that they would one day be frolicking in his pool, he wouldn't have believed them.

Silence filled the room once Austin finished telling Zoe about Janna and the role she once played in his life. He'd never intended to hurt Zoe, but talking about a past love made him realize even more how unfair it was to have proposed to any other woman. Memories of Janna had often invaded his mind, holding him back from fully giving his heart to anyone. Sharing everything with Zoe, he realized how much Janna still meant to him.

But he had no intention of risking his heart to Janna again. Yet he couldn't help but wonder if Janna had been correct in saying that it was fate that brought her back into his life.

"I don't know what to say." Zoe stood and stepped away from the counter they were sitting at. Austin stood, too. She folded her arms, her hands moving up and down them as if trying to get warm.

"None of this was planned. I haven't seen Janna in years, and I never stepped out on you while we were together."

"I know." She looked up at him, tears pooling in her eyes. "I never should have agreed to marry you."

Ouch. Austin flinched at her words.

"I think, in the back of my mind, I always knew there was someone else."

"There wasn't—"

"Yeah, there was. Janna might not have been around physically, but she was always in the middle of our relationship," Zoe spat out bitterly, but she quickly harnessed her temper. So like her. Always in control of her emotions. "I'm not trying to go all clinical on you, but subconsciously you have never gotten over her. And no other woman will ever stand a chance until you either see where things end up with you and Janna, or you let her go. For good."

What could he say? Zoe was right. Question was, was he ready to put it all on the line for another chance with Janna?

Chapter 8

Janna stuffed her wet bikini into her bag and zipped it. Grateful that Austin had an outdoor shower and changing room near the cabana, she had taken full advantage of them after swimming a few more laps. Sitting on the deck, she placed her bare feet up on the railing and lounged, enjoying the beautiful evening. Every so often she would try to listen to see if she could hear Austin and Zoe, but Janna heard nothing. At least there wasn't any screaming and glass crashing against the walls. She didn't know who this woman was to Austin, but considering she had a key to his house and he had a photo of her on his mantel, it was safe to say she meant something to him.

"And the fact that he's left me out here for almost twenty minutes speaks volumes," she mumbled in the stillness of the night.

She lowered her feet and slipped back into her sandals. She moseyed over to the guesthouse, which was a few yards from the cabana, hoping the door was unlocked. During dinner, Austin had mentioned that he did his woodworking there. If she knew where the heck she was beyond the suburb of Johns Creek, she'd call a cab.

Trying the handle, Janna smiled when it turned and she pushed the door open. Feeling against the wall, she searched for a light switch. She should feel guilty about invading his private space, but she didn't. As far as she was concerned, when he left her out there alone, he gave her free rein to check everything out.

After she found the switch, the room was immediately bathed in light. She stood frozen in place. This was some guesthouse. From where she stood, it looked larger than her first apartment.

She turned back and closed the door before roaming around the space. The open floor plan revealed a cute little kitchen with a long eat-at counter that overlooked the living room. If it belonged to anyone else, she would have considered the space a man cave, with the large-screen television mounted on the wall and a host of electronics in a nearby corner. The huge leather furniture took up most of the space.

Janna glanced back at the door before heading down a hallway. She passed a full bathroom but stopped at the first open door. Flipping on the light revealed Austin's workshop. As she moved farther into the room, it seemed as if he had knocked down several walls to create a massive area. Woodworking equipment, lumber and a few finished pieces filled the bulk of the space.

"I see you found my workshop."

Janna whirled around, her heart racing. Austin was leaning against the doorjamb.

"You scared me." Her hand rested against her chest.

"Sorry about that."

"I hope you don't mind—" she pointed her thumb behind her "—but I decided to show myself around, since you were *occupied.*"

"I don't mind," he said quietly, his gaze steady on her.

Janna turned away from him and continued her perusal of the space. "Bookcases, huh?" She risked touching one that was lying on two drying horses, hoping it wasn't still wet, but curious nonetheless.

Austin pushed away from the door. She had noticed right away that he had showered and changed. A vision of him wet with his visitor popped into her head, but she quickly shook the thought free. The last thing she wanted to do was imagine him with someone else.

"I started with small items like jewelry boxes, birdhouses and such. Then it was chairs and benches. Lately, it's been bookcases." He ran his hand down the side of one that was standing upright near the back wall.

"What do you do with your finished products?"

He shrugged. "Give them away or donate them to various organizations."

"Well, from what I see in here, if you ever decide to give up your day job, you can definitely make a living making furniture. Your pieces are beautiful. It's remarkable that you can add such details without a whole lot of equipment."

"Thank you." He turned to her and stuffed his hands into his pockets. Again he stared at her and she couldn't figure out what he was thinking.

"So I assume she's someone special to you," Janna said of Zoe. He had to know she was going to ask questions.

"My ex-fiancée."

"Fian...fiancée?" Janna stammered. She didn't know what she expected, but it wasn't that. "You have a fiancée?"

"Ex-fiancée."

Now she was the one staring. He had always wanted to marry and have a family. But the fact that he'd been close to marrying someone other than her left her mind reeling.

He removed his hands from his pockets and rubbed the back of his neck as he approached her. Draping his long arm around her shoulders, he turned off the light in the room and guided her back to the front of the cottage-like house.

They sat on the sofa in silence until he said, "I was never really in love with her."

She lifted an inquiring brow to him, but remained silent. He said the words as if that fact explained everything.

"We started off as friends, and though I cared for her, I was never in love with her."

"Then why'd you ask her to marry you?"

"I *thought* I was in love...and I was ready to settle down. Or at least I figured I was. She broke off the engagement."

"And how did you feel?"

"Zoe said I was incapable of really committing. I had asked her to marry me, but I could never agree on a wedding date. After six months of being engaged and still no date set, she told me she couldn't marry me. We recently broke up. She believed that there was something holding me back, something in my past."

"Was she right?" Janna held her breath.

Austin slumped forward, his elbows on his thighs. He rubbed the back of his neck again as the silence between them grew.

"I denied it," he said, staring down at the floor, "but she didn't believe me. And she was right not to."

He glanced over his shoulder at Janna, and her heart was pounding so hard in her chest, she had no doubt that he could hear it. The love she saw brimming in his eyes showed way more than what he was saying.

"I never stopped loving you, but—and I hate to say this—I tried. God knows I tried." He sat back on the sofa and stretched his arm behind her without touching her. "What I felt for you was so unbelievably powerful."

Janna knew she shouldn't be doing a happy dance inside, but she was glad to hear that she wasn't the only one suffering emotionally during their years apart.

He sat back against the sofa and draped his long arm behind her.

"Not many days went by that I didn't think of you—" he ran his hands through her damp hair "—yearn for you. I couldn't seem to let my memories of you go."

She so wanted to ask how he felt about her now, but she didn't dare. Instead she turned in her seat, propping one of her knees on the cushion when she reached for one of his hands and said the first thing that came to mind.

"Just think. Your ex-fiancée caught you frolicking in the pool with a supermodel."

He chuckled. "Be quiet and kiss me."

He gently yanked on her hand and pulled her into his lap. He cupped her face and lowered his head. The kiss started sweet and gentle, but the heat between them grew into a roaring fire. She felt promises of new beginnings with every nip of his teeth and every swirl of his tongue.

Emotions she had only ever felt with him came rushing back with force. Without breaking contact, she straddled him, placing one hand on the back of his head and holding him close as she ground against him. His hands lowered to her waist.

What did all of this mean as far as she and Austin were concerned? Janna knew the type of chemistry they shared didn't come along every day, and she so wanted to see where this deep attraction could take them.

She pulled back to catch her breath and Austin slipped his hand to the tail of her T-shirt, lifting the flimsy garment over her head. Janna's nerves were getting the best of her as it felt like the first time. The first time she'd made love with the man she cherished more than anything.

Austin laid her back on the double-width sofa and hovered above her, his eyes blazing with passion. She wanted him so badly she was tempted to pull him down on her and have her way with him.

"You are absolutely the most beautiful woman I've ever laid eyes on." His desire-laden voice washed over her like a cool breeze.

Going braless definitely made for easy access. Janna forced herself to let him get his fill of her bare breasts as his gaze raked down her body. He lowered his head and snaked his tongue out over a pert nipple and Janna practically leaped out of her skin. A wave of lust rushed through her body when he paid the same homage to the other breast. Sucking, licking—his mouth had always done wicked things to her.

When he lifted his head, she quickly helped him remove his shirt, tossing it to the side. She wanted him more than a starving woman wanted food and she couldn't wait. Her gaze took in all of him, from the way his broad shoulders tapered down to a narrow waist and his rock-hard abs. Her hands moved up the side of his smooth body and rested again on his chest, where his heart hammered a staccato beat beneath her touch.

"You're even more magnificent than I remember." She tweaked his taut nipples, chuckling when his body jerked and he swore under his breath. He grabbed her hands and lifted them above her head, holding them in place while his mouth covered her breast. An electric current gripped her.

"Austin." She rocked her hips beneath him, wanting to feel more of him.

Heat rushed through her veins and she knew she couldn't take much more of this seductive scene. It had been too long. Too long since a man made her body hum with need and too long since a man made her feel so desired.

Austin groaned and with a hand on her left hip halted her movements. He placed a soft kiss on her nose, on her chin and then another against her lips before he lifted himself slightly. He must have seen the question in her eyes—*Why'd you stop?* He pushed all the way up and grabbed both their shirts from the floor.

"Put it on," he said, clearly frustrated when all she did was look at the garment. He slipped his over his head. "I want you more than I've ever wanted any woman in my life, but I don't want to rush this. I don't want us to have any regrets."

Regrets? Hell, the only regret she was having at the moment was the fact that he had stopped. Irritation coiled inside her gut as she jerked her shirt over her head and stuffed her arms through the sleeves. She'd suffered years of not having him in her life. There was no way she would have second thoughts about them finishing what they had started.

"I remember our first time. Do you?" he asked quietly.

Janna exhaled a small breath and glanced up, staring into his gentle eyes. A peace like she hadn't felt in years suddenly settled over her at his words. She would never in her life forget their first time. How could she? It was the single most astonishing day of her life.

"Very few women can actually say that their first time was with the man they loved. A man who made them feel like the most important person in the world.

A man who took his time and worshipped her body as if she was some type of priceless gem. But I can."

She'd been sixteen and they had been dating for a year and a half. His parents had gone away for the weekend, leaving him and his brother home alone. Austin had invited her over for brunch. He had cooked everything from pancakes to salmon croquettes, all to impress her with his culinary skills.

She smiled up at Austin and kissed him.

"I had never been so nervous in all of my life." He chuckled. "I knew early on that you were the one for me, the one I had planned to spend the rest of my life with."

The smile that had only moments earlier covered his mouth slipped as he lowered his eyes. Janna prayed he wouldn't bring up how she left or how she had tossed their future away.

Instead he said, "I didn't want to disappoint you, knowing it was your first time."

Her heart melted.

"You definitely didn't. You were gentle, thoughtful, and I felt safe. Most importantly, I felt loved. Never disappointed." If she were honest, she would have to admit that she'd wanted him to make love to her well before then. They had come close a number of times, in his car, at the park and even in his parents' den when they weren't home. But he had always put the brakes on before things went too far. Like tonight.

His smile returned. "I'm glad to hear that." He slid his arm behind her neck and pulled her close, placing a kiss on the top of her head. "I never want to disappoint you, which is why I stopped what we were about to do."

"I don't understand."

"If we start this…whatever this is between us, with sex, I'm concerned it will screw any chance of us having more, and I want more. I want us to spend some time together, get to know each other again. If that's okay with you."

She wanted to say that he could get to know her after they were reacquainted with each other's bodies, but she didn't. She hadn't been intimate with a man in almost a year, and she'd never been with anyone who meant as much to her as Austin did. She had to admit, she wanted more, too.

Chapter 9

Austin whistled as he walked down the hall toward his office. After two meetings that involved hashing out budgets for a couple of the firm's biggest projects, normally he would be ready to call it a day. Not today.

For the last week and a half, he and Janna had spent every day together. Dinners at his place, movie marathons that included action flicks, long talks over wine, and some serious kissing sessions that only stoked the sexual tension between them. Her presence in his life made him realize just how much he had missed her.

"Hi, Austin. I see you made it back," Beverly, his secretary, greeted him when he stepped into the front office. She stood and handed him his messages. "Nice tie."

Austin absently ran his hand down the length of the

gift Janna had given him a few days earlier. He tended to wear designer ties, but he had a feeling the multi-colored silk neckwear exceeded even what he would normally pay for one.

"Oh, and Janna Morgan called and said she should be here around noon," Beverly said. Austin glanced at his watch, noting that it was twenty minutes till. "I didn't realize you knew the supermodel. It's going to be great to meet her."

"Yeah, we grew up together. I'll make sure I introduce you two." Actually, he was sure Janna would introduce herself upon arrival and make Beverly fall in love with her the way everyone else did.

Fall in love. He had never stopped loving Janna, but his feelings for her now had risen to a whole different level.

He turned from Beverly's desk to head to his office.

"Oh, and your brother is waiting in your office."

"Okay, thanks."

Austin stopped in his office doorway and frowned at seeing his brother sitting in his chair with his feet on his desk.

He closed the door. "Don't you have an office of your own?" He swiped his brother's feet down. "Get up."

Malcolm took his time standing. At just over six feet tall, he was a few inches shorter than Austin. They had the same build and probably weighed close to the same, but personality wise, they were on opposite ends of the spectrum.

"Yeah, I have my own office, but can't I come and hang out with my little brother sometime?"

"Only when you want something." Austin stood at his desk and sifted through the messages Beverly had given him. "So what do you want?"

"Your secretary was right. That is a nice tie." Malcolm dropped down in one of the guest chairs. "As a matter of fact, it doesn't look like anything you would pick out for yourself. I'd say that beautiful supermodel you've been spending so much time with is trying to bring you into the twenty-first century with your style. Thank goodness."

Austin shook off his suit jacket and hung it on the back of his office chair before sitting down. The way he felt about Janna, she could do whatever she wanted to him. He didn't know what he was going to do when she headed back to New York in three days. He wanted to beg her to stay in Atlanta with him, but she was at the apex of her career. He couldn't put her in a position to choose between him and her job again.

"There you are staring off into space again," Malcolm cut into Austin's thoughts. "It's a wonder you've been able to get any work done with Miss Hottie in town."

Austin sat back in his seat and folded his hands on top of his head. "Are you in here for a reason? Because if you're not, feel free to show yourself to the door."

"As a matter of fact, I am here for a reason." His brother turned serious. "What would you need from me in order to increase my department's budget? I thought we could go another year with the CAD/CAM, the computer-aided design and manufacturing system, that we have, but I don't think so. Ours is so outdated,

I think we're going to have to upgrade sooner rather than later."

Despite his brother's partying ways, Austin had to admit that Malcolm was the best building designer. As the director of that department, his brother was brilliant when it came to thinking outside the box and offering their customers unique and fresh ideas.

"Do like everyone else is required to do, submit a request."

"I can do that, but brace yourself. This system is not cheap."

A knock on the door interrupted their conversation. "Come in."

The door swung open and a gust of adrenaline swept through Austin like a bullet from a high-powered rifle. He didn't think he'd ever get used to the sight of Janna.

Those seductive eyes. That smile that lit up his life. And that body. *God, that body.* It was no wonder he hadn't been able to think straight these last few weeks. Dressed in a red blouse with a plunging neckline and fitted jeans with her signature ponytail, she had his body tightening with desire. Hell, she could wear a burlap sack and still have him drooling. He fought the desire to march across the room and take her right up against the far wall. He couldn't do that. Not only because Malcolm was in the room, but also because he wanted their first time back together to be more romantic—and on a bed.

"Good afternoon, fellas." She closed the door and strutted into the room with all the confidence of a woman who was used to being the center of attention.

Austin's gaze went to the picnic basket in her hands.

Funny how he hadn't noticed it when he first spotted her in the doorway. She carried it as if it were an accessory to her outfit, and damn if she didn't make it work.

He and Malcolm stood.

"Hey, beautiful," Malcolm said, greeting her with a kiss on the cheek before Austin could get to her. "Surely by now you know you're hanging out with the wrong brother, right?"

She set the basket down on a nearby table and cast smoky eyes on Austin. "Mmm, I think I have the right one."

Austin stepped around the desk and she walked into his open arms. He covered her mouth and kissed her with enough passion to let her know for sure that she had the right brother and how glad he was to see her.

Once he let her up for air, she said, "I definitely have the right brother."

Malcolm chuckled. "I guess that's my cue then. I'm outta here."

Austin ignored his brother and captured Janna's lips again, eliciting a moan from her that spurred him on.

"Don't mind me. I'm just going to go and get back to work," Malcolm said as he left the office.

"I thought he'd never leave," Austin mumbled against Janna's mouth. "But I'm glad he did."

He rested his forehead against hers. "Hi."

She grinned. "Well, hello."

Stepping out of his hold, she lifted the picnic basket. "Ready?"

"Uh, yeah, but I didn't know we were going on a picnic." He glanced down at his clothing. "I had planned on ordering lunch in. That way we could eat while we discussed more of your business plan."

"Yeah, about that. I forgot to bring it."

His eyebrows shot up. "I thought the whole point of lunch was to work on it."

"Well, that wasn't the whole point of lunch," she said seductively. She walked up to him, her hands against his chest and her lips a breath from his. "I also wanted to see you."

"Is that right?"

"Yep, and I wanted to do this."

Her mouth settled over his, and he suddenly didn't give a damn about lunch or anything else for that matter. *Strawberry lip gloss*, he realized when he tasted her lips again. A wave of nostalgia washed over him. Like years ago, he was powerless to resist anything she offered. Her hypnotic scent floated around him, weakening his defenses even more.

He thrust his tongue into her mouth greedily and knew that a kiss today wouldn't be enough. He wanted all of her. His hands made contact with bare skin when they went to her waist, pulling her closer so that she could feel the effect she was having on him. *Smooth*, *soft* and *warm* were the words that came to mind when his hands traveled up her back beneath her blouse.

Oh, yeah, he definitely wanted more. He needed more.

Breathing hard, he broke off the kiss. "Maybe we should just skip lunch and take this back to your place."

"What about work?" she asked. A glimpse at her kiss-swollen lips turned him on even more.

"It'll be here when I get back."

* * *

Twenty minutes later, they were barely able to get inside Janna's hotel room before they were ripping each other's clothes off.

"I've never seen this side of you," Janna said, panting and shimmying out of her jeans as she backed her way toward the bedroom with Austin following. She had already tossed her top and they were leaving a trail of clothes and shoes along the way.

When Janna stood just inside her bedroom door in only her skimpy red lace bra and panty set, it was as if time stood still. Austin was less than a yard away in his black boxer briefs, looking like an Adonis.

Janna's heart rate kicked up as she took in all of him. *Beautiful everywhere*, she thought as her gaze landed on him. No doubt national magazines would fly off the shelves if Austin's perfectly sculpted body was featured on the pages. Exquisitely built, from his wide shoulders down to his thick muscular legs, and he was hers.

"Wow," she finally said, the word tumbling out of her mouth. He moved forward, visibly admiring her lingerie with each step he took. It was the same heated look that was brimming in his eyes when he'd all but ogled her skimpy white bikini.

"Wow, yourself."

She squealed when he swept her up into his arms and carried her to the bed. He threw back the covers, holding her as if she weighed nothing, and laid her down. Before joining her, he placed several foil packets on the bedside table. She hadn't realized he'd had them in his hand, but a ball of excitement bounced inside her gut, knowing that they were really going to do this. She'd wanted him weeks ago, but knew the wait would be worth it.

When he turned to her, his eyes blazing with desire, she squirmed under his watchful gaze as his fingers traced a seductive path from her neck down to the center of her chest. Experienced fingers unclasped the front of her bra and she quickly shrugged out of it.

Excitement pumped through her veins when he palmed her breasts, tweaking and teasing her nipples. Her breath hitched when his tongue replaced his fingers on one nipple, rotating and teasing the hardened bud before moving over to the other.

Janna's eyes drifted closed and her body squirmed beneath him as he kneaded her breasts, sucking and tugging as she groaned in pleasure. His teeth grazed a sensitive peak, sending an erotic sensation scurrying from the top of her head to the pads of her feet.

"Austin," she breathed. "I don't know how much of this I can take."

His hands continued torturing her breasts as if she hadn't spoken while he kissed a fiery path down her body, not stopping until he reached the top of her bikini panties.

"Though you look hot as hell in these, they have to go." Before she could blink, he had slid them down her legs and was back to torturing her with soft kisses against her heated skin. Gone was the boy who was nervous about making love to her as a teen, and here was a man who knew what he was doing. Knew what he wanted.

He raised his head, his hands roaming down the sides of her body. "You're gorgeous with clothes on, but without them, you take my breath away. Absolute perfection."

His gaze stroked every inch of her and Janna had to fight her natural instinct to strike a pose. She remained still as she lay vulnerable under his heated perusal. She wanted this so badly. She wanted him…all of him.

He sat back on his haunches, his hands still caressing her body. He had that look in his eyes. The same look he had when he brought their intimate moment at the guesthouse to a halt.

"Don't even think about stopping this," she said with attitude, his gaze holding hers. "I'm not the shy girl you once knew and I plan to have my way with you this afternoon."

Austin chuckled. "Baby, there has never been a shy bone in your body." He stood suddenly and removed his boxer briefs.

Janna's mouth dropped open and the smart retort teetering on the end of her tongue froze. When she compared him to an Adonis earlier, she hadn't seen what lay beneath his briefs. *Magnificent.*

"As for you having your way with me, I'm all yours."

From his words, his tone and the look in his eyes as he stared at her from the foot of the bed, Janna knew he was talking about more than just this moment.

"And I'm all yours," she murmured, barely able to breathe as he slowly climbed back on the bed, the muscles in his body contracting with each stealthy move toward her.

Her thighs fell open of their own accord as if inviting him in, but Austin would not be rushed. He lifted her foot, turning it in his large hand, and placed a kiss on the inside of her ankle. She whimpered as he slowly made his way up her leg, covering her skin with his sweet kisses.

"Austin," she said, her voice barely above a whisper as his mouth caressed the inside of her thigh. Her stomach tightened and an orgasm teetered on the edge of her control.

It didn't take much for her to reach that point when Austin's experienced mouth did wicked things to her body. His tongue joined in on the fun and passion raged deep inside her core. Her eyes slammed shut. "I can't hold…" She fisted a handful of the sheet in her grasp and her hips lifted off the bed as her sex throbbed with need. "I want you in…inside me."

Austin lowered her leg and slid a finger inside her slick heat.

"Oh, baby," he said on a husky groan, adding another finger, sliding in and out of her hard and deep. "You're definitely ready for me."

"Austin!" she screamed, her hips bucking with each thrust until waves of ecstasy pushed her over the edge of her control and into a hysteria of delight.

Austin wanted to make her come over and over again, and today he planned to. His pulse pounded wildly as her erotic sounds filled the quietness of the room. His own control was hanging by a thread as he watched her come all over his fingers.

She whimpered and her eyes opened at half-mast when he removed his fingers. Grabbing one of the foil packets from next to the bed, he quickly sheathed himself.

"I wanted to take this slow, but…" With a hand on either side of her head, he nudged her thighs wider and entered her in one smooth move.

Janna's legs trembled as her interior walls fisted around his shaft. A blast of pleasure shot through him at the heat their joined bodies generated.

Austin cursed under his breath, knowing this round was about to be over way before he wanted it to, but she felt so good. Damn good.

Oh, yeah, this was worth the weeks of waiting, he thought as he picked up the pace. His thrusts grew faster, harder and he went deeper, losing himself in her sweet heat. She matched him stroke for stroke as he increased the speed.

He gripped her hips and plunged even deeper. Her body trembled in his grasp and her nails dug into his shoulders.

"Au…Austin," she whimpered her breathing more ragged, her moves more jerky. "I…I'm…" Her words stalled when another orgasm ripped through her and she screamed his name.

Austin held on to her soft flesh, knowing he was right behind her. One last thrust and desire tore through his body, sending his world into a turbulent tailspin. He growled her name as an explosion of fiery heat sent him over the edge of his control.

Collapsing on top of her, he held her tight as he struggled to catch his breath. Totally spent, but not wanting to keep too much of his weight on her, he rolled onto his back.

"That was mind-blowing," Janna said, still gasping for air when Austin pulled her into his arms.

He placed a light kiss against her damp forehead. "Yes…yes, it was."

Chapter 10

Janna lay tucked against Austin's side, his arm around her and his hand resting on her hip. She'd had a feeling that when they finally came together it would be explosive, but the reality exceeded her fantasy.

"You're awfully quiet. Are you okay?" Austin shook her gently.

She lifted slightly and smiled up at him. "I'm better than okay. I thought my first time with you was special, but this was beautiful."

He watched her, his eyes barely open. "I agree." He rolled her onto her back and sat up, resting his weight on his elbow while staring down at her. "I have missed you so much. Being with you again, and like this…doesn't seem real. I never want to lose you again."

Excitement bubbled inside Janna. Her vacation was

quickly coming to an end and for the last few days all she could think about was the two of them.

"So what happens now?" she asked, her hand caressing the smooth skin of his solid chest.

"You mean, after I make love to you again?" He grinned, wiggling his eyebrows up and down.

She laughed. "No, silly. You know what I mean. What happens now…with us?"

"What do you want to happen?"

"I want *us* to happen. I know getting back to what we once felt for each other might take some time, but I don't want what we've had these last couple of weeks to stop just because we live in different cities."

Though she knew without a doubt that she was in love with Austin, she wasn't sure how he felt. Janna knew she had hurt him, but she wanted another chance for them to rebuild what they once had.

"I agree," he said, breaking into her thoughts. Austin fluffed one of the pillows and placed it under his head, his attention still on her. "But I have to be honest. I have never considered a long-distance relationship. It's hard enough maintaining a connection when you live in the same town as the other person. Living in different states will pose some challenges."

"I guess we'll have to figure out how to do this so that it isn't so hard."

"I don't want it to be hard, either, but I know anything worth having is worth working for. I'm ready and willing to do whatever it takes. What about you? Are you willing to put in the work?"

"Definitely. How about if I start now?" She threw

off the sheet covering their naked bodies and struck a seductive pose.

He threw his head back and laughed. "Works for me."

The next morning, Austin sat in his office thinking about what he wanted for his future. His father had started grooming him from his first day in college to one day take over the business. But that's not what Austin wanted long-term. Numbers and finance had always come easily to him and he enjoyed his job, but the CFO position wasn't something he wanted forever. He had always enjoyed working with his hands and preferred to be in the trenches with the tradespeople they employed, working with wood.

Now that Janna was back in his life, something else was on his mind. Marriage and a family. That's what he wanted with her. Unfortunately, after a failed engagement—two, if he counted his youthful proposal to Janna—he didn't trust himself when it came to matters of the heart. But deep inside his soul, he knew Janna was the woman for him. What he felt for her was like nothing he had ever felt for anyone. He was in love with her, but could he trust her? Could he trust her not to toss his love away like she had before?

His cell phone rang, pulling him out of his musings. "Hello.

"Hi, handsome," Janna crooned, bringing an automatic smile to his face.

"Hi, yourself. Where are you?"

"I'm at the hotel now. I just had lunch with Macy

and then I went by her medical complex. I haven't been there since the grand opening and can I just say that your company did a beautiful job. The building is marvelous."

Months ago, Reynolds Development had completed a project spearheaded by Macy and her husband, Derek. Macy had always dreamed of opening a medical complex and Derek, an architect, worked up the designs. They had commissioned Reynolds to renovate a seventy-five-thousand-square-foot building. The day of the grand opening had been when Austin spotted Janna from a distance. Little had he known that Macy and Derek were related to her.

"I'm glad you liked the building. So how's your sister doing?"

"She's great, and as expected, I had to suffer through her talking about her pregnancy all during lunch. But I'm happy for her. She's an awesome mother to Jason and Amber. Having another baby only seems fitting since she's wanted a family like…forever."

Austin listened as Janna talked about her siblings. Besides rehashing the plans that they'd made in the past, he and Janna hadn't discussed marriage or having a family yet. He wasn't sure if she wanted either. Though that was a path he wanted to take, right now Janna's career was her priority. Besides, they had only been dating a few weeks, way too early to be thinking about marriage.

"Are you sure you'll be able to get the next few days off in order to spend this Memorial Day weekend with me?" Janna asked, pulling him back into the conversation.

"Positive. I was even able to get a seat on your flight."

"Even better!"

It worked out that he had some business to attend to in New York, and he planned to spend a few extra days there with Janna.

"I'm so glad you're going back with me. I have a photo shoot Friday morning, but the rest of the weekend, I'm all yours. Except there is one thing."

Austin kept himself from groaning. With Janna, that one thing could be anything. "Okay, I'll bite. What is it?"

"Will you be my date for a dinner party that Vera Wang is having Saturday night? I know you hate stuff like that, but I promise, it won't be that bad."

Austin shook his head and smiled. There wasn't much he wouldn't do for her, even attend a party where the topic of conversation would be fashion.

Days later, Austin carried their luggage into Janna's Fifth Avenue penthouse. The two-story unit had spectacular views that could be seen through the wall-to-wall windows clear across the room. She had told him that she could even see Central Park.

Leaving the bags in the foyer, she gave him the grand tour of the four-bedroom, five-bathroom apartment.

In his line of work, Austin had seen his share of grand places, but he had to admit Janna's stood out more than most. From the architectural details to the stunning scenery beyond the windows, she had definitely chosen a gem. Considering all the traveling she did, he wondered when she actually had time to enjoy the place.

"This is my second-favorite space in the house," she said of the kitchen.

Austin laughed. "I'll admit it's incredible, but why is it your favorite when you don't even cook?"

"Because I like to eat."

He shook his head, finding that just as funny, considering she ate like a bird. He walked around the eat-in kitchen, taking in the oversize stainless steel appliances as well as the cabinets of the same material, some with doors, others without. The unusual beige-and-tan backsplash caught his attention as well as the white dishwasher that stood out like red paint on white carpet.

"So what's your favorite room in the house?"

"My bedroom." She grinned. "Come on. I can't wait to show you. You're going to die when you see my closet."

Austin laughed again, unable to help himself considering her excitement. He dropped his arm around her shoulders and placed a kiss on top of her head. Her enthusiasm was contagious. The last few weeks had been filled with plenty of laughs, a lot of fun, and her companionship was second to none. At some point, they would have to spend some time apart since she had to get back to work and he would eventually return to Atlanta. But until then, he planned to enjoy his time with her and live a little.

"Okay, so what do you think?" Janna asked once they finished the tour and returned to the living room.

"I think the space is almost as beautiful as you are."

He pulled her into his arms. "Almost." His lips touched hers, but before he could deepen the lip lock, the doorbell rang.

Janna groaned. "Don't go anywhere. I'll get rid of whoever it is."

"You do that, and in the meantime, I'll take these bags to the bedroom."

Janna looked through the peephole and sighed when she saw her visitor.

She swung open the door.

"What are you doing here?"

"Hello, Janna. Welcome back. May I come in?"

Janna stepped back and Nelson Heath walked in as if he owned the place. Tall, lean and impeccably dressed, Nelson had a presence about him that made both men and women take notice whenever they occupied the same space.

She gave him a once-over. It seemed as if she wasn't the only one who had taken a little vacation. His spiked blond hair and tanned skin looked as if he had gotten a little sun recently. Even at fifty-five, he didn't look a day over forty.

"What can I do for you, Nelson?" Janna moved past him and walked back into the living room, knowing he would follow. She sat on the sofa and he rested in the upholstered chair across from her.

Nelson typed something into his handheld device. "I figured we could get an early start discussing some assignments that—"

"You do remember that I fired you, right?"

He looked up and frowned. "What? You were serious?"

"As a heart attack. Do you have any idea what you did to me? To Austin?"

He set his tablet on the small round table next to him and crossed his legs, showing off argyle socks in the same colors as his shirt.

"I know I kept a sixteen-year-old safe. I know I jump-started your career, ultimately making you a successful model in a seriously competitive industry. I also know that I made both of us very wealthy. Okay?"

His cockiness grated on her last nerve.

"But you also ripped me away from the only man I have ever loved, and that's not okay."

"Janna, love, I was responsible for you. Not just for your safety, but also your well-being. I did what I thought was best. You were a child. If I had to do it all over again, I would make the exact same decision."

"Well, it's a good thing you won't get the opportunity to do it all over again." Austin's deep voice filled the space and Nelson leaped out of his seat, his hand on his chest.

His surprised expression would have been comical had this not been a serious situation.

"I take it this is Austin Reynolds," Nelson said once he recovered. "The man you've been playing kissy face with while in Atlanta."

"Be careful, Nelson." Janna stood next to Austin. Nelson might have been almost like a father to her over the years, but she wouldn't stand for him belittling or disrespecting either of them.

She and Austin had already talked about her not seeking out a new manager and giving Nelson another chance. But she'd figured she'd let her manager stew for a while, knowing he wouldn't give her up without a fight. By showing up at her place before she could settle in, his actions were as she predicted. They'd had their share of disagreements over the years and she'd fired him a number of times. He always came back days later as if nothing happened. And she always took him back.

"I'm sorry, all right? I owe you both an apology."

"Yeah, you do," Austin said and snaked his arm around Janna's waist. "And for the record, we might have been young, but we were very clear about our feelings for each other."

"The only way I'll accept you back in my life, Nelson, is if you promise to never do anything like that again. Austin means everything to me. If you ever come between us again, you'll be very sorry."

Janna had no intention of letting anyone or anything interfere again. Ever.

"Drop your head back slightly and tilt it toward me so that I can get a glimpse of the diamond-studded earrings in this shot," the photographer said to Janna and he snapped shot after shot.

For the past hour, Austin had watched as Janna showed why she was one of the most sought-after models in the industry. She smiled, smirked and at times laughed out loud during the photo session as if she were having the time of her life. Most times the photographer let her do her own thing and just took pictures. She was clearly in her element.

The photographer stopped and pointed out a few things on his computer screen to Janna.

"I'll have the contact sheet available later. If you want, I'll let you take a look at the proofs before I send them over to the client," he said.

"Kenny, you're the best," Janna gushed and hugged him. "I know you don't do this for just anyone, but thanks for looking out."

While they talked, Austin watched her as she gave her opinions about the various frames. Some days he still couldn't believe she was back in his life. And in the two days they'd been in New York, she'd shown him how invested she was in her career. He'd already known how hard she worked, but for the past day and a half, he'd witnessed it.

The photographer took a couple of additional shots as per Janna's request. Austin's heart swelled with pride. She was exquisite. He didn't even want to think about what the world would have missed out on had she not pursued this career choice. The plans they had made years ago were good, but he could honestly say he was glad she'd gone after her dream. It would have been selfish of him to not share her, that gorgeous face and her beautiful spirit. His mother often said that anything meant to be would be, and he now knew Janna was meant to be a model.

"Hey, baby." Janna walked up to him and threw her arms around his neck, planting a noisy kiss against his mouth. "I'll probably need another hour. Do you want to stick around?"

He had come directly from having breakfast with a potential client to the studio, unable to go another minute without seeing her. Yes, he was tired after a week of submitting proposals and reworking budgets, but being with her always gave him extra energy.

"I'll wait."

"So what do you think about all of this?" She waved her arms around at the space.

"I think it's cool, and I think you're absolutely amazing." He kissed her lovingly. It was as if he hadn't just seen her hours earlier. He couldn't wait to get her alone.

"You say the sweetest things."

Instead of responding, he kissed her again. With that gesture he wanted her to feel everything he felt for her without having to utter a word.

"Wow, you must be really happy to see me." She smiled sweetly once he let her up for air. "Oh, and I want a repeat of that when we get out of here. I should be done soon and then I'm all yours."

Austin watched her walk away. The gentle sway of her hips was hypnotic, soul stirring. This woman, this sweet, sexy, dazzling woman, was his. He felt so blessed that they'd been given a second chance, and every day he fell more and more in love with her. The strong feelings he still had for her didn't freak him out as much as they had weeks ago. In fact, the thought of having to leave her in a couple of days made him feel ill.

Austin stepped over to the industrial-size windows and stared down at the busy Manhattan traffic. After several business trips there in the past year, New York was starting to grow on him. The energy, the glamour, the endless amount of things to do—all of it was slowly seeping into his bones.

Now that Janna was back in his life, it was starting to look even more appealing. He'd never thought he could do a long-distance relationship. Actually, he'd never wanted to, but after spending those weeks in Atlanta with Janna, he couldn't bear the thought of letting her go. Not knowing how things would progress or if they could make this work, he had to try.

He turned from the window and watched as she posed for the camera. He wanted forever with her.

But did she want the same thing? He hadn't asked, for fear of her thinking that he was moving too fast. The last thing he wanted to do was scare her off by discussing forever too soon.

Chapter 11

Austin sat in awe. It seemed as if his mouth hung open most of the evening whenever Janna strutted down the catwalk at the charity fashion show. Even after four months of dating and traveling to New York, experiencing life in her world, she was still able to surprise him.

She paraded to the end of the stage, her confidence shining through like a beacon in the night, commanding and holding the attention of everyone in attendance. She made a few twists and turns, showing off the intricate design of the garment she was wearing. His heart galloped when she struck a pose, smiled brightly and winked at him before turning and heading back. That's when his heart stopped completely. The serious dip in the back of the dress plunged to the top of her perfectly round ass, almost showing way more than he was comfortable with everyone seeing.

He stuck his finger between the collar of his shirt and neck, trying to loosen the suddenly tight fit. She had to know what effect the outfit would have on him. He didn't dare look around at any of the other men in attendance, sure that they'd had the same reaction.

Before he could recover from the previous outfit, she returned, wearing an equally provocative pantsuit. Though it covered a little more of her body, it was clear that she wasn't wearing underwear.

Maybe attending a fashion show after not seeing her for two weeks wasn't a good idea.

He sat in a constant state of arousal each time she stepped foot on the stage. He had arrived in New York a few hours ago, unable to get an earlier flight. They'd only had a few minutes to squeeze in a quickie before she had to leave for the fashion show. Even with that release, his body was wound tighter than an oil drum, and he couldn't wait to get her all to himself.

When all of the models stepped out on stage for the grand finale, the crowd erupted in applause. He was clapping and whistling louder than any one. Granted, the show was awesome, but he couldn't wait to get the hell out of there so that he could worship Janna's exquisite body.

After months of dating, everything was working better than he could have imagined. As he was a planner by nature, there wasn't a day that went by that he didn't think about their next steps. He wanted more, yet he hadn't figured out how they both could get what they wanted. But he would.

As agreed, Austin waited for Janna in the foyer of the elegant hotel, surrounded by people dressed as if they should have been in the show. The more Austin experienced Janna's world, the more he was convinced that she was doing exactly what she was meant to do.

"Hey, baby. I saw you clapping and whistling. I guess you liked the show." She kissed him before giving him a chance to respond. This was probably her way of keeping him from saying anything about her skimpy outfits, and damn if her distraction wasn't working.

"I loved it," he said when she ended the kiss.

"I knew you would." She looped her arm through his. "We have to hurry. I want to stop home real quick before we head to the after-party."

Twenty minutes later, Austin had to admit that he'd thought her reason for wanting to stop home was to finish where they left off earlier. In each other's arms. Instead, he was sitting in one of the upholstered chairs in her bedroom, waiting for her to finish changing into something more appropriate for the after-party.

He dropped the magazine he was sifting through and sat back, stretching his legs out in front of him. His eyes drifted closed. If she didn't hurry up, he would be out for the count. No sooner than the thought crossed his mind, he heard the bathroom door open.

"Well?"

His eyes grew large and he sat speechless.

The slim-fitting dress that stopped just above her knees had open, two-inch squares that started at the sides of her breasts and went down each side of her body. The sexy outfit, with the deep V in the front and the back, barely covered her assets and would definitely catch attention.

"Well?" she asked again, impatience in her voice. She twisted and turned again to give him another look, as if he hadn't already memorized every inch of the garment.

"I think I'm not letting you out of this apartment."

Janna stopped moving and looked at him as if trying to determine if he was for real.

"You're not serious."

"The hell if I'm not! You have fifty million dresses in that store you call a closet. I'm sure you can find something that's a little less...less," he stuttered, "no, not less, but something with more material. A lot more. Every man with a pulse will be drooling over you in that dress."

Janna strutted up to him, smiling. "Sometimes you drive me nuts with your overprotectiveness, or is it possessiveness? At any rate, you sure are cute when you're all riled up."

He frowned, not appreciating the fact that she wasn't taking him seriously.

"Just think, with me in this dress, hanging all over you tonight, you'll be the envy of every man at the party." She gave him a quick peck and ignored the low growl as she walked away to put the finishing touches on her look. "Oh, and by the way, I'm not wearing any underwear."

The air was electrified with energy when they pulled up to the warehouse-like building, one of the hottest spots in the city. The nightclub often booked some of the world's most famous DJs, and no doubt Grand Master Rock-It had already started turning it up. Janna could hear the music all the way outside.

"Are you sure you're up for this?" she asked Austin when he helped her out of the vehicle. Limo after limo pulled up to the building, dropping off some of America's most famous people.

"About as ready as I'll ever be," Austin grumbled, making a face that almost made her laugh out loud. He was such a trouper. The day had been a whirlwind and she had yet to welcome him back to her city the way she wanted to. A quiet evening at home would have been nice, but she had already committed to the charity fashion show and after-party. Besides, she was dying to wear her L.J. Owens original. It was a gift from the up-and-coming designer for agreeing to do the show at the last minute. Considering he was donating 40 percent of the proceeds to a charity that supported foster children, she couldn't refuse.

"Come on. Let's dance."

Janna pulled a reluctant Austin to the middle of the floor as soon as they stepped into the establishment. He knew how to dance. It just wasn't something he necessarily enjoyed.

The moment they found a good spot, the music changed to a slow jam.

"Now this is what I'm talking about," Austin said huskily and pulled her against his body. "I've been wanting to have you rubbed up against me since seeing you step out on that stage in that first outfit."

Janna smiled up at him and looped her arms around

his neck. She loved being close to him. She loved him.
He had yet to say those three magic words, but his actions spoke just as loudly. Janna was pretty sure they felt
the same about each other. She just wished he'd say it.

"God, you smell good." Austin nuzzled her neck as
they moved in perfect sync, as if they'd been dancing
together forever.

"Thank you. And may I say, you're looking sexy as
hell in your tux."

"Sexy enough for you to want to go home right now
and rip it off me?"

She threw her head back and laughed. "Yep, but
we're not leaving yet. I will say, though, when I get
you home, it's on." She gave an exaggerated wink, eliciting a laugh from him.

Oh, yeah, she planned to have a real good time with
him.

Austin felt as if he'd been gritting his teeth for the
past hour as he escorted Janna around the multilevel
nightclub. Every eye had been on them from the moment they stepped through the door. No, make that the
moment Janna stepped through the door. He'd admit
that she looked good—damn good—but having so
much attention on them had him holding his breath
most of the night.

They strolled past a wall with floor-to-ceiling mir-
rors and he groaned inwardly at their reflection. She
was clearly trying to give him a heart attack by wearing the too-revealing, too-tight, too-damn-sexy dress.
And to tell him she wasn't wearing any underwear was

downright cruel. It was taking every bit of willpower he had not to pull her into the nearest broom closet and have his way with her.

Janna tugged on his arm and he leaned close in order to hear her over the music that seemed to get louder by the minute.

"Why don't we go up to the VIP lounge? It's not as crowded and we'll be able to hear each other without yelling over the music."

"Sounds good. Lead the way."

Austin had never been the type to react to seeing famous people, but the A-listers in attendance did make him take a second glance. Though it was childish, he couldn't wait to brag to his brother about not only seeing, but meeting, some of their favorite actors.

"Now, isn't this better?" Janna said when they arrived in the area that was less crowded and definitely not as noisy.

"Much." He didn't bother asking her why she had just suggested it. He knew. Tonight she wanted to be seen. Supposedly the guy who designed her dress was the next big thing in fashion and her new favorite designer.

Though Austin had been taken aback by the dress she was wearing, he was tempted to commission the guy to make Janna a few more outfits. For his eyes only, of course.

"Do you want another glass of wine?" Austin asked, his hand at the small of her back, his mouth only inches from hers.

"That'll be nice, but someone should be walking

around with…" Her voice trailed off and she stiffened next to him.

"What's wrong?" He squeezed her waist and then followed her gaze.

"What is she doing here?" she ground out a heartbeat before the second most beautiful woman Austin had ever seen approached them.

"Hello, Janna."

"Phoenix."

Chapter 12

Āll Janna could do was stare at the woman who gave birth to her. She shouldn't have been surprised that she would show up, but she had hoped their most recent encounter would have been their last one.

"It's nice to see you," Phoenix said, vulnerability in her eyes. "I love your dress."

Had Phoenix been anyone else, Janna would have said the same to her. The soft blue strapless maxi dress with the deep side split, which appeared to be Versace, was absolutely stunning. Instead, she said, "Thank you." And snapped her mouth shut to ensure she wouldn't say something she'd regret later.

"Can you give us a moment?" Phoenix asked her date, a man young enough to be her son. Janna had seen him at a few events in New York but didn't know his name.

Phoenix glanced at Austin as if expecting him to leave them, but Janna touched his arm before he could move away.

"Please stay," she said to Austin, but she wasn't compelled to introduce them. "Phoenix, we have nothing to talk about. Your appearances and your need to say anything to me are starting to get a little old."

"Janna, why are you doing this?" Her voice was low and almost pleading. "I just want us to be friends, but you won't even accept any of my phone calls."

"That should be a clue that I don't want to talk to you. As a matter of fact, like I've said on more than one occasion, I want nothing to do with you. Why can't you just accept that?"

"Because I'm your mother!"

Anger pulsed through Janna's veins. "You are not my mother," she ground out between gritted teeth, feeling Austin move closer. She inched toward Phoenix and whispered, "The day you relinquished your parental rights was the day you became dead to me."

Phoenix reared back as if she'd been slapped, her hand quivering against her chest. Janna was almost taken in by the hurt in the woman's eyes. Almost. She wasn't fooled. Phoenix was a world-renowned actress and no doubt she was putting on her best performance.

"I was so young," she said softly, her voice raspy with emotion. "I couldn't raise a child on my own. I tried. God knows I tried. But once you started school, it was too much…too hard to juggle waitressing and casting calls. I had no family. There was no one I could count on to help me. I thought I could get myself together and come back for you, but—"

"But you didn't," Janna spat. "Instead you abandoned me in foster care and then gave me away!"

"Janna." Austin placed his arm around her waist as her voice rose.

"If that wasn't a clue that you wanted nothing to do with me, changing your name nailed it home."

"Okay, that's enough," Austin said quietly near her ear and tried steering her away from Phoenix.

"You're right, that is enough," Janna said of Austin's comment. She returned her attention to Phoenix. "Just stay away from me."

Janna allowed Austin to guide her through the VIP section and to the stairs. She fought the strong urge to hide her face, sure those nearby had heard the conversation. She had been trying so hard to change her image. Trying to show the world that she was more than a pretty face, but also a woman who had a good head on her shoulders and could make a difference in the world. Yet, those few minutes might have wiped out any progress she had made.

Austin dropped his arm from around her waist and reached for her hand, carefully guiding her down the stairs. Once they reached the bottom step, he pulled out his cell and called for their car. Janna just wanted to go home and not show her face for at least a month, but that wasn't possible.

Once they reached the lower level, no one paid them any attention as Austin shouldered through the dancing crowd. The music, excruciatingly loud, did nothing to drown out the thoughts roaring through her mind. Thoughts about how she had just told the woman who had given birth to her that she was as good as dead to her. Thoughts that she had caused a scene that was sure to end up on someone's front page. And thoughts that brought a rush of tears to her eyes.

Just hold it together. Just hold it together, she chanted in her mind. She held her head back, blinking rapidly, knowing that if one tear fell, others were sure to follow.

Austin didn't stop moving until they were outside. People were still arriving and fans were hanging out, hoping to see their favorite stars. Austin hurried her off to the side where their car had dropped them and waited.

She glanced up at him and he didn't say a word. Instead he opened his arms to her. Unable to hold back any longer, she buried her face in his chest and sobbed.

"How do you feel?" Austin asked when he removed the empty mug from her hand and set it on the bedside table. They had returned to Janna's place an hour ago, but she still looked as if she'd just lost her best friend.

"I feel okay," she mumbled and scooted farther down into the bed. Austin sat next to her and gently pushed a few loose strands of hair away from her forehead.

"You don't sound okay."

Silence. He sighed and leaned forward, his elbows on his thighs. Austin didn't know what to say to make her feel better. There were so many things he wanted to ask regarding the announcement that Phoenix Hudson was her mother. *The* Phoenix Hudson. That was like having Denzel Washington as his father. The thought of that would be mind-blowing. He couldn't believe Janna had never told him.

"I'm sorry," she sobbed, wiping feverishly at the tears on her cheeks. "I'm so sorry you had to witness that. I just hate…"

"You just hate what, sweetheart?" He rubbed his hand over her back in small circles, hoping to provide some comfort.

"I just hate the way you had to find out who my birth mother is…and I hate the way I spoke to her."

Austin had to admit he almost didn't recognize Janna tonight. Her tone, her mean words and even her demeanor were so uncharacteristic of the woman he knew. The woman he had fallen in love with all over again. He couldn't pretend to understand how it felt, knowing that your mother gave you up to pursue her career. He only hoped he could somehow help her move past the hurt.

"I'm sick of being in the media in an unfavorable manner. I don't even want to think about what's going to show up in a rag magazine this week," she groaned and flipped on to her back, the sheet barely covering her breasts.

Austin mentally chastised himself for even noticing where the sheet fell. All evening he had imagined peeling that skimpy dress off her and indulging in all the freaky positions his mind had fantasized about.

"Do you think she was there to stir up drama?" Janna asked. "To get attention? She does have a new movie coming out."

"I don't know, but honestly, I don't think so. She

genuinely looked like a mother who was desperate to talk to her child."

"She's not my mother!" Janna spat out. "She left me for her career. Tossed me away as if I meant nothing to her. I just don't understand that. I don't understand how a mother can do that. Mama Adel would never do anything like that…no matter what Hollywood was offering."

Austin didn't want to bring up the fact that Janna had done the same thing to him. Tossed his love away like a bag of trash in pursuit of a career. Granted, it wasn't the same, seeing that he and Janna had been just kids. But still.

Austin leaned over and placed a kiss against her lips.

"Why don't you try and get some sleep?"

"Aren't you coming to bed?"

"Yes."

Austin kicked off his shoes and pulled the tail of his shirt out of his pants. He quickly undid the buttons and started on his belt when Janna spoke again.

"Can you go a little slower? I want to watch."

Austin shook his head and laughed, glad her sense of humor was still intact. The situation with her birth mother wasn't over, but they would get through it. Together they could get through anything.

The next morning Janna cracked open her eyes and stretched her arms wide, accidently bumping a sleeping Austin. A smile tipped the corner of her lips and she turned onto her side to face his body. He'd done an incredible job taking her mind off the situation with

Phoenix. Going to sleep and waking up with him by her side was something she wanted to do every day. She had no idea what their future held, but she'd give anything to spend the rest of her life with him.

Lying on his stomach, Austin had his head buried in the pillow and his thick arms hugging it. Janna could watch him all day. She rose up on her elbow and ran her hand slowly over his back. With smooth skin the color of toasted almonds, his broad back and muscular arms were only a few of his physical attributes that she loved.

Her hand moved to his lower back, where the sheet rested over his firm butt. She knew he worked out three times a week, but he had a body that looked as if he put in hundreds of hours at the gym. Her hands went lower, but the intrusive sound of her cell phone interrupted her mini-excursion and broke the silence in the room. Austin groaned next to her and snuggled farther under the covers.

Part of Janna wanted to ignore the phone, but in light of what happened the night before, she thought it best to at least see who was calling.

She hurried across the room to answer it.

"Hello," she whispered hoarsely, seeing that it was Nelson. Who else would call her at six in the morning? By this time, he was probably on his second cup of coffee and had been at the office for an hour.

She grabbed the silk robe draped over a chair in her sitting area and hurried out of the bedroom, closing the door behind her.

"Janna, what the heck happened last night? Is it true that Phoenix Hudson is your mother? Tell me it isn't true and that I'm not being blindsided by the top news of the century!" he yelled.

She could picture him pacing feverishly in front of his desk, running his fingers through his hair. She really should've given him a heads-up last night, but by the time she arrived home, the last thing she'd wanted to do was talk to anyone who wasn't Austin.

"It's true that she's my birth mother. Not my mother."

Silence filled the phone line and again Janna could picture Nelson's reaction. No doubt he had dropped down in his desk chair, his eyes closed and his fingers pinching the bridge of his nose.

"No. No. No. This is not happening. How could you not tell me something like this? I've known you for ten years. How the hell has this not come up? You've had plenty of times to say, 'Hey, Nelson, by the way, my mother is Phoenix frickin' Hudson!' Oh my God, Janna! Are you kiddin' me?" he roared.

She didn't bother responding, knowing he wasn't done with his rant, but once she thought he was done, she filled him in on the details.

"I should have known. I…should…have…known. You're both drop-dead gorgeous with perfect cheekbones and bodies that would make a gay man drool. I should have seen the resemblance. I can't—"

"Nelson. Nelson!" Janna had enough. It was too early in the morning for this. "Nelson?"

"What?"

"Did you call me for any other reason? Because if not, I think we can have this conversation later. Like, say, after twelve noon."

"Come on, Janna! We have to pull everyone together for damage control and figure out how to spin this crazy, awesome development. Do you know what this is going to do for your career?"

"Okay, that's it. Goodbye, Nelson. I don't feel up to talking about this right now." She hung up, not giving him a chance to debate. It figured he'd be excited by the news.

"Is everything okay?" Austin asked, standing at the entrance into the living, his sleep-filled voice sending delicious shivers through her body. Wearing only a pair of blue silk pajama bottoms, he looked hotter than a soldering iron in an oven.

"Yeah, everything is fine, baby. That was Nelson. I didn't get a chance to ask him how he found out, but apparently news has broken about me and Phoenix."

"Sweetheart, I'm sorry." Austin strolled across the room and sat on the sofa next to her, pulling her into his arms. He placed a kiss against her temple and laid his head back, clearly not fully awake.

Janna loved how peace consumed her whenever she was in his arms. With him, it felt as if all was well in the world. But she knew otherwise. The shit had hit the fan and it hadn't even been twenty-four hours yet. She didn't dare turn on the television. At any minute, Mama Adel and her sisters would be…

She didn't get a chance to finish the thought before her cell and landline started ringing.

"I think I'm going to scream…or cry," she groaned against Austin's chest.

The phones eventually stopped ringing, only to start again.

"If you're not going to answer those, can we go back to bed?"

"If I don't answer, everyone is just going to keep calling."

"In that case…" Austin leaned forward and dropped his arm from around her. He lifted her cell from the table and silenced it before stumbling across the room to the house phone. He picked up the cordless and pushed a few buttons before setting it back down.

Surprised by his actions, Janna just sat staring at him, appreciating how he was taking charge.

He extended his hand to her. "Come on. Let's go back to bed. You can talk to everyone when you're ready, but right now I'm going to take advantage of having you all to myself."

Chapter 13

"Mama, I don't know what to do," Janna said to Mama Adel. Whenever she didn't want to get advice from her sisters, she could always call her mother. They could talk about anything without her passing judgment. "Last night, I lost it when I saw her, and then when she blurted out that she was my mother I snapped."

Mama Adel was quiet for a long moment before speaking. "Janna, there's something I need to tell you. Though I promised Phoenix I'd never share this, I think there's something you should know about her."

Janna stopped pacing and dropped down in the nearest chair. Somehow she knew her mother was going to say something she didn't want to hear.

"Phoenix and I have been keeping in touch since you were five years old. When you were my foster child, the system didn't allow it, but I knew she was sincere about making sure you were well taken care of. Once I adopted you, we talked more often. That was also when she started getting bigger movie roles. She would send me money for you. For clothes, your schooling, anything you needed, she was right there to support."

Janna had always wondered how Mama Adel was able to afford her private school. And this information explained why they'd been able to move into a four-bedroom, two-bathroom house in one of the nicer neighborhoods in Edison.

Janna's chest tightened. She had always thought that Iris and Macy had been sending money to help with the household expenses. Now the more she thought about it, the more other things started to make sense.

"Baby, I'm so sorry I didn't tell you, but Phoenix asked me not to. So please understand, just because she wasn't there for you in the flesh every day, you were never far from her thoughts."

"I don't know what to say." All these years she thought that Phoenix had given her away and hadn't looked back.

Nausea swept through her body as everything she'd said to Phoenix the night before came flooding back.

"Oh, Mama, I really put my foot in it this time. You wouldn't believe some of the things I said to her."

Her mother chuckled. "Actually, knowing how you felt about her, I can just about imagine."

"I have to fix this."

"Yes, you do."

Shortly after ending the call, Janna found Austin sitting in the living room watching *SportsCenter*. It was months into their long-distance relationship and they'd gotten into a comfortable routine. Austin made the trip to New York at least two or three times per month, since his schedule was more flexible than hers.

Janna stood back and observed him, loving how relaxed he seemed in her space. This was what she wanted—them together forever, but preferably living under one roof. She had often dreamed of what it would be like to have a family of her own, even more so after Iris and Macy married. What would it be like if she and Austin were to marry and have a few children?

Austin turned slightly and their gazes met. "Hey. Is everything all right?"

"Well, that depends on your definition of all right."

She moved across the room and plopped down next to him. Tucking her legs underneath herself, she snuggled next to him and told him about the conversation with her mother.

"There was something I realized while talking to Mama Adel."

"What's that?"

"I'm a hypocrite. I've been so busy punishing Phoenix for leaving me for her career that I didn't realize I had done the same thing to you."

Austin remained quiet. Janna assumed he had already thought the same thing. How could she have not seen it sooner? She could argue that the situations were different, but ultimately she'd put her career before the man she loved.

"I owe both you and Phoenix an apology."

"You don't owe me anything, Janna." Her head was resting on Austin's shoulder and she looped her arm through his. "We agreed months ago to put the past behind us and start fresh. Besides, after seeing you in action during your photo shoots and the fashion show, you made the right decision. You were born to be a model and I'm proud that you grabbed hold of the opportunity."

She lifted her head. "But it was at the expense of what we had."

"I know, but we got a second chance. Let's not look back." He dropped his arm from around her. "Now, what are you going to do about your moth— I mean, Phoenix?"

"I'm not totally sure. There's a short video clip floating around with me and Phoenix arguing and there were witnesses who said they heard her say she was my mother. Nelson is working with my publicist and has been in contact with Phoenix's people to determine how to spin all of this."

"Yeah, I get that, but before you and Phoenix go public with anything, you need to have a conversation with her. The two of you have to make peace and decide what type of relationship you want."

"I know," she moaned. "I just don't know what I'll say to her. She's been trying to reconcile for the last couple of years. Though I'm still a little peeved about how she left me, I feel awful about how I've treated her."

"Well, how about this? How about if I cook dinner and you invite her over here?"

Janna's heart swelled. "You would do that for me?"

"Sweetheart, do you have any idea how much I love you? There's nothing I wouldn't do for you."

Janna's heart rate kicked up and she thought the organ would explode in her chest. She'd never thought she would ever hear Austin utter those words again.

"I love you, too."

He lowered his head and kissed her sweetly. All the anxiousness and doubt she had been feeling drifted away like a feather in the wind. She felt like the luckiest woman in the world, but then Austin halted their kiss way before she was ready.

He caressed her cheek with the back of his fingers. "Besides, cooking dinner for two very beautiful women would be my pleasure."

Janna grinned and then sobered. "Thank you…for everything. I don't know what I would have done if you hadn't been here with me."

"You would've been fine, but I am glad I was here." He stretched his long arms up and yawned. "Okay, so I guess we should make a move. If you can get Phoenix over here, you'll be able to apologize to her on your turf, away from prying eyes. Except for the ton of media camped outside the building, that is. They'll see her come in, assuming she'll show, but at least your conversation will be private."

Hours later, Janna paced near the kitchen counter, where Austin was putting the finishing touches on a tossed salad.

"Would you relax?" He reached out and pulled her close. "Everything is going to be fine."

Janna sighed against him. "I know, but I didn't think

I'd be this nervous." She had changed clothes at least three times, something she rarely did. She had finally decided on a soft pink cashmere cowl-neck sweater, which she paired with slimming black jeans. "I just hope she can forgive me."

"Considering she agreed to come by, I think you're off to a good start."

The doorbell rang and Janna shivered against Austin.

"You'll be fine." He placed a quick kiss against her temple. "Now go get the door before she changes her mind and leaves."

Janna swatted him on the arm and laughed. She really was glad he was there to support her.

Hurrying down the hallway, she stopped briefly for one last glance in the full-length mirror inside the first-floor bathroom. Satisfied with the way she looked, she went to the door.

"Hi, Phoenix."

"Hi, Janna. I hope I'm not too early."

"You're right on time. Please come in." Janna stepped aside, admiring the strapless silk jumpsuit Phoenix was sporting. They definitely had similar taste in clothing.

Janna led her to the sofa and sat next to her.

"I have to tell you, I was surprised to get your call."

"I can imagine," Janna mumbled, sliding her sweaty palms down her jeans-clad thighs, unsure of what to say now that she had her there. She'd lucked out that Phoenix hadn't flown back to Los Angeles, her home, yet. "I owe you an apology."

"And I owe you one. It's my fault that we're the topic

of conversation on every talk show today. I shouldn't have blurted out that I'm your mother. I just… I just…"

"You just got caught up in the moment. I know the feeling. I said some horrible things to you."

"Janna, you have every right to be angry with me. I wasn't there for you. I couldn't be the mother you needed."

"Actually, I found out this morning that you *were* there for me. I talked with my moth— I talked to Mama Adel. She told me what you did for me. What you did for us. Can you ever forgive me?"

Phoenix waved her off. "There's nothing to forgive. I'm so glad you had someone like Adel. Heck, I wish I had someone like her." She chuckled. Janna's heart went out to Phoenix, knowing that she didn't have any family besides her. "I can't begin to tell you how many times I called her for advice."

For the next forty-five minutes, they talked about their individual lives, their careers and Austin. Feeling comfortable with the conversation, Janna told her how she and Austin had gone their separate ways and run into each other again months ago.

Janna had to admit that talking with Phoenix was like talking with a girlfriend. Sure, they had some work to do on their newfound bond, but Janna felt hopeful that everything would work out.

She looked up to find Austin standing in the doorway that led to the kitchen.

"Are you ladies almost ready for dinner?"

"I can't believe he cooks, too," Phoenix said in a conspiring whisper, and Janna burst out laughing.

"Somebody in this relationship has to know how to cook." Janna stood. "Shall we eat?"

Austin sat listening to the two women laughing and talking as if they'd been friends for years.

"Austin, dinner is fabulous," Phoenix said, cutting into her meat. He had prepared roasted chicken with balsamic bell peppers, brown rice, and a tossed salad.

"He's an awesome cook," Janna added.

"Thank you, ladies."

They went back to talking and Austin took the opportunity to observe. He couldn't believe that he'd never noticed the resemblance before now. Other than Janna's cinnamon-brown skin tone versus Phoenix's café au lait complexion, they could almost be twins. Both had oval-shaped faces, big, expressive eyes, prominent cheekbones and long hair with highlights. Their senses of humor were also similar.

Austin took a swig from his beer. He liked seeing Janna happy, which was most of the time. Yet, this evening, she had a special glow. The fact that she bounced back from disappointment so quickly was one of many qualities he admired about her.

His mind flashed back to earlier when he'd told her he loved her. She'd seemed taken aback by his words. Surely she had to know he was in love with her. He might not have said the words before, but he knew. After that kiss she planted on him at the fundraiser, he hadn't been able to stop thinking about her. His father's story about how he'd fallen in love with Austin's mother came to mind. Like him, all it took was a kiss to remind Austin that Janna was the one for him.

"So, Austin, Janna told me you're a financial genius."

Austin grunted. "I don't know about all of that."

"He's being modest."

"Have you ever considered a career in financial management? Branching out on your own?"

"It crossed my mind in college, but I decided to join the family business after graduating. Yet, who knows—" he shrugged "—it might be something I'll consider in the future."

"Well, if you do, maybe I can be your first client," Phoenix said.

"Actually, I'll be the first," Janna piped in and leaned over to kiss him.

Before she pulled away, he lifted her chin to stare into her eyes. "You'll always be first with me."

Chapter 14

"It's not often an old man gets to spend a Friday night with his two sons," Patrick said.

Austin had to admit that this was a rare occasion. He enjoyed hanging out with the two of them, but rarely did they do so at a bar. Of course it had been Malcolm's idea. And if Austin had to venture a guess, he'd bet his paycheck that soon it would be just him and his father. Malcolm was scoping out the small space and by the looks of it, he had plenty of women to choose from.

"Looking for someone, son?" Patrick asked Malcolm.

"Always," he said absently.

Austin and his father made eye contact and smiled, both thinking the same thing—that they were going to be abandoned at any minute.

"I assume things are going well with you and Janna?"

his father asked. He was sitting in the middle between Austin and Malcolm.

"Better than okay." He thought about the small velvet box in his pants pocket. He had picked up the five-carat Asscher-cut diamond ring a couple of hours ago and felt as if he were carrying a brick.

He wasn't sure why he was so nervous about proposing to Janna. No, actually, he did know. His judgment when it came to dating, as well as asking women to marry him, wasn't that good. Sixteen-year-old Janna and then Zoe might have said yes, but here he was, still unmarried. Those relationships weren't meant to be when he thought about his feelings for Janna now. But after two failed engagements, he wanted to be sure he was doing the right thing.

"You two want another drink?" his father asked.

"I'll have a beer." Austin raised his almost empty bottle.

"What about you, Malcolm?" Patrick asked.

"Actually, I hate to do this to you guys, but I see someone I know." Austin followed Malcolm's gaze across the room, noticing where a woman sat in a booth alone, staring at his brother. "Thanks for the drink, Dad." He lifted his glass of bourbon and walked away.

"He stuck around longer than I thought he would," their father said.

Austin laughed. "I know, right?"

"But getting back to you. It's been, what, five or six months that you and Janna have been seeing each other?"

"Five." Five amazing months. Austin's only complaint was that he didn't get to see her as often as he'd like. A few times a month wasn't nearly enough.

"What are your intentions with her, if you don't mind me asking?"

"I don't know, Dad. No, I do know, I'm just not sure."

"About what?"

"I'm not sure if I'm ready to propose marriage to her. You know my track record when it comes to relationships. I don't want to keep repeating the same mistakes. I think… I feel that Janna is the one. For real this time."

His father chuckled and brought his glass of scotch to his lips. "I can see why you would be a little gunshy about another proposal. Is there something you feel with Janna that you didn't feel with Zoe?"

"Everything." He shook his head, in awe of what Janna had brought to his life. "She's like a breath of fresh air. She always makes me want to throw caution out the window and try new, more daring things."

"I have seen changes in you these last few months. You seem happier. You're not staying at work until the wee hours of the morning, and even the way you're dressing has changed." His father nodded toward his attire. In the past, Austin would have on a suit, but on Fridays now, he usually wore a polo shirt with dress slacks or jeans. The changes had come gradually, and he had to admit, he liked the new, more comfortable look.

"Yeah, I feel different with her in my life again. She makes me feel as if I can leap tall buildings in a single bound." They laughed. "Just talking to her on the phone, my world seems brighter. Heck, just thinking about her makes my heart rate skyrocket."

Austin took a drag on his beer, surprised he had shared that much with his father. They had always had a great bond, but they'd never talked this candidly about any of the women in Austin's life.

"I'll tell you, women who make you feel powerful and cherished at the same time don't come along every day. Sounds like she might be the one."

"What do you think? Does it take more than those feelings to know for sure if this is the woman I'm supposed to spend the rest of my life with? How do I know for sure if I should propose marriage?"

For a person who had always considered himself intelligent, he was clueless in this area.

"Follow your heart, son. There are no guarantees. If it feels right, go for it. We're all living on borrowed time. Snatch up any happiness you can get—it sounds like Janna is the woman who makes you happy."

"And she's the first person I think about when I open my eyes and the last person I think about when I close my eyes at night," Austin said, recalling the conversation he'd had with his father months ago. "She's the person I see myself growing old with. The person I see as the mother of my children."

The only thing he wasn't sure of was if she saw him in the same light.

Nelson had called Janna all excited earlier, claiming he needed to see her immediately. She had no idea what was so urgent, but considering he had been on his cell phone since arriving ten minutes ago, it couldn't have been too important.

She left him in the living room while she headed to the kitchen for a glass of juice. She'd been on an emotional roller coaster the last few days. Austin had arrived three days ago and she wanted to spend every moment with him, especially since she hadn't seen him in two weeks. But he was distracted. She wasn't sure if it had to do with her nonprofit, his work or something else. The good news he'd given her the day he arrived was that all the paperwork for Precious Home was complete and they should know about the 501(c)(3) status any day now.

Janna knew that she wouldn't have accomplished half as much had it not been for his help. Every day she fell more and more in love with him. She knew him, which was why she knew something was wrong. When she asked, he'd claimed it was work. One of the projects outside New York was over budget and they were having some issues with the client.

It's more than that, Janna thought to herself. He wasn't expected back into the city until later and she was determined to get him to open up to her once he returned.

"Okay sorry, love." Nelson strolled into the kitchen with his tablet in one hand and his cell phone in the other. "I didn't think that call would take that long."

"So what's going on? What's this big news you wanted to talk to me about?"

"How do you feel about Milan?"

She frowned at him. "You know I love Milan. Actually, I love Italy, period." The country had a special spot in her heart since it was where her career started. "Why do you ask?"

"Your favorite fashion designer in Italy is starting a new line, and he wants you and Phoenix Hudson to be his muses. He wants you two to be the faces of this collection."

Janna's mouth dropped open. *This is a first.* She listened as Nelson explained the initial concept of the assignment and how it would also include some runway modeling, as well as commercial work.

"So what do you think?" Nelson's excitement was contagious. Afraid that she would be too hasty in making a decision due to the elation pumping through her veins, she sat in one of the kitchen chairs.

"I think all of this sounds wonderful. I can't believe you've been working on this for three months and never said anything."

"Some of their ideas were still up in the air, but I wanted to make sure I kept your name out there. And when the news broke about you and Phoenix, they tweaked their original ideas and the negotiations began."

When he told her how much she'd make, she almost fell out of her chair. Granted, she had enough money to feed a small country for the next thirty years, but more couldn't hurt. The thought of doing something she loved in a country she adored with people she enjoyed working with was a bonus. Then there was Phoenix. She and Janna had been talking and spending time together over the last couple of weeks. Now they would get a chance to work together, which could be fun.

"You'll have to commit to a year of living in Milan."

Unease swept through Janna, and she dropped back against her seat. "A year?" she said quietly. Austin immediately came to mind. Her gaze dropped to the promise ring and she absently twisted it around her finger. "If you brought this opportunity to me a year ago, I would have jumped at it." But now her decisions didn't just affect her. She and Austin were making things work, but going back and forth to Milan would definitely cause some challenges.

"So is that a no?"

"I didn't say that."

"Then what are you saying?"

"I'm saying I have to talk to Austin about all of this before I can make a decision."

"Janna," he said in that frustrating tone.

She gave him a warning glare, daring him to say anything negative. He and Austin tolerated each other, but she didn't see them ever being good friends.

"You're going to have to tell me something soon, real soon. The start date is November first, and it's already mid-September."

Part of her wanted to say yes immediately, knowing that offers like this didn't come along often. But that other part that was madly in love with Austin wanted to say no without even telling him about the opportunity. She couldn't lose him again. And then there was her nonprofit. Would she be able to manage everything from so far away?

Janna folded her arms on the table and rested her head on them. This would all be so much easier if she knew where she and Austin stood. She wanted a happily-ever-after with him, but what would happen with her career? Her life was finally falling into place. With his help, she had a great team of financial advisers. And thanks to some changes in her personal life and her relationships with Austin and Phoenix, her media image had improved significantly. People in the business world were taking her seriously when she talked about her nonprofit.

Was she willing to risk any of that?

Austin froze. The words *Milan* and *year* screamed through his mind. He hadn't intended to listen in on their conversation, but before he reached the kitchen's entrance, he heard those words.

He took a few steps back and ran his hand over his mouth and down his chin. Taking a breath in and releasing it slowly, he tried to slow his pounding heart. He had only heard a small portion of the conversation, but enough to know that Janna had an opportunity in Milan that she had to make a decision on. *Milan*. Of all places.

What the hell was he going to do? He didn't want to lose her, but the thought of traveling back and forth from Atlanta to Milan was unsettling.

This news definitely put a wrinkle in his special plans for the evening. He finally decided to ask for her hand in marriage, and this popped up. *Damn.*

Once he got his heart rate down and drowned out some of the thoughts running rampant through his mind, he stepped into the kitchen doorway. Nelson was leaning against one of the counters, his back to the door, and Janna was sitting at the kitchen table with her head down.

As if sensing his presence, she lifted her head and their eyes met. Though she looked tired, that beautiful smile that lit up his world appeared.

"Hey, baby." She rose and he moved farther into the kitchen, meeting her halfway. "You're back early. I didn't hear you come in." She kissed him on the lips and he wrapped his arms around her in a hug, placing another kiss against her temple.

"I just got here," he said, his gaze meeting Nelson's. He wasn't a fan of the guy. He also didn't necessarily trust him, but he did believe that Nelson had Janna's best interest in mind when it came to her career. "Are you okay?" he asked Janna when he felt her shiver in his arms.

"Yeah, I'm fine." She slowly moved out of his arms, the smile gone from her lips.

"Well, I guess I'll leave you two. Janna can tell you about her once-in-a-lifetime opportunity in Milan," Nelson said. Austin didn't miss the way Janna scowled at her manager when he placed a kiss on her cheek.

"How did things go with your client?" Janna asked when she returned from seeing Nelson out.

Austin leaned against the counter, his arms folded across his chest. "Everything went okay. We were finally able to reach an agreement that all parties could be happy with."

"I'm glad to hear that." She rinsed a glass and placed it in the dishwasher.

Austin could tell she wasn't ready to talk about the

Milan opportunity. If he had to be honest, he wasn't sure he was ready to hear about it.

"So I guess you're probably wondering what that was all about with Nelson," she said quietly, keeping some distance between them. Normally when they shared a space, she was right up under him.

This is not good. This is not good at all.

"I'm interested, but let me take a shower and then we can talk."

Minutes later, Austin stood in the shower under the powerful spray, his eyes closed, unable to slow his mind down. All he could think was that he couldn't lose Janna. They had a second chance to get their re-union right, but how could they do that thousands of miles apart?

He placed his palms against the ceramic tile of the double-wide shower, and with a heavy heart, he lowered his head and let the steamy water run down his back. He didn't want to do long distance anymore with Janna. If he asked her to stay in the US, marry him and possibly move to Atlanta, she might. But would she feel as if she was the one giving up everything? He could move to New York and travel back to Atlanta maybe every ten days.

He released a noisy groan and stood upright. His hands covered his face and he let them slide down, wishing the move could clear his mind. There was no sense in thinking about this any longer until they talked.

"Austin?"

Austin opened his eyes at the sound of Janna's voice. He hadn't heard her enter the bathroom. His gaze took in her nude hourglass figure standing an arm's reach away and his mouth went dry.

"Can I join you?"

He didn't speak. He answered her question by extending his hand and gently pulling her to him.

"I needed to be close to you."

"I love having you close."

She was probably the only black woman he knew who didn't seem to mind getting her hair wet. But instead of her being directly under the shower head, he turned her and backed her against the opposite wall of the shower.

"I love you." The strain in his voice was noticeable to his own ears, but he couldn't help it. Emotion clogged his throat. He stared into her eyes, braced a hand on the ceramic tile near her head, and caressed her cheek with his other hand. "I love you so damn much." Between each word, he planted kisses on her cheek, on her neck and even on her shoulder.

"I love you, too."

His hands moved to the back of her head, and he covered her mouth with his. He didn't only want his words to express his feelings, he wanted to show her. He wanted her. He needed her. His life would be hell if he had to live without her.

Thoughts of what they were going to do about Milan left his mind, and all his attention was on the woman in his arms. Their kiss started like a light summer breeze, but she wasn't having that. Janna pulled him closer, taking what she wanted. A frisson of heat shot through him as their kiss turned into a hunger he couldn't ignore.

Austin groaned into her mouth. His hands palmed her firm butt, lifting her off the tiled floor. A kiss wouldn't do. He wanted all of her.

Janna wrapped her long legs around his body and moved against his erection. A whole new wave of desire enveloped him as he slipped inside her. He was glad that she was on the Pill because at this point, he wouldn't be able to stop even if he wanted to.

Lifting her up and down his length, he went deeper. Harder. Faster. With every thrust, he wanted her to feel his love. With every thrust, he wanted her to know how much he cherished her. With every thrust, he wanted her to know he couldn't live without her.

Janna snatched her mouth from his. "Austin," she breathed, clawing his shoulders. Her head was thrown back and her body tightened around his shaft. It took everything in him to keep them upright. If she kept moving the way she was, this would be over just as fast as it started.

Feeling as if he was losing his grip, he pressed her back against the wall but didn't stop pumping in and out of her. He couldn't stop. Fire burned through his veins, and her soft whimpers spurred him on.

When his mouth made contact with her neck, she lost it. Her body jerked and clenched with an orgasm that almost brought him to his knees.

He didn't stop. His impending release built with every thrust into her warm body. She climaxed again and he lost it. Growling her name as his orgasm toppled him over, sweetly draining all of his concerns.

He slowly lowered her feet to the floor of the shower,

their panting mingling together. He kept an arm on her hip, still trying to catch his breath.

Her arms tightened around his neck and she buried her face in its curve. That's when he heard her sobbing.

He tried pulling back, but she wouldn't loosen her grip.

"Baby, what is it? Did I hurt you?"

"No." She shook her head against his shoulder, her wet hair brushing against his face. "I just love you so much. Sometimes it feels overwhelming," she whimpered.

Yeah, I know, he thought to himself.

A while later, Austin and Janna sat at the dining room table, eating dinner. Candles lit every flat surface, and in some respects, Janna was enjoying the evening. Unfortunately, there was a little twinge of foreboding nipping at the back of her neck.

After their shower, they'd slept for about a half an hour. Well, she slept. She wasn't sure if Austin had fallen asleep. When she woke up, she found him downstairs, setting the table and putting out the dinner that he had ordered from her favorite Italian restaurant.

Now they were eating a delicious meal, surrounded by candlelight. The evening was very romantic, but a sense of dread had been nagging her during most of the meal.

"So by accepting this opportunity, you would get to work with Phoenix?" Austin asked and lifted his wineglass to his mouth.

Janna nodded.

"That has to be exciting. Not that the rest of the job doesn't sound like a once-in-a-lifetime opportunity." He used the words Nelson had earlier. Janna could have choked her manager. His parting words were meant to force her hand into talking with Austin.

"Baby, I don't have to take it. I love what we have going here and I don't want anything to come between us, especially a job."

He said nothing and fear crawled up her spine. She knew he was thinking about how she'd left the first time for Milan, because she was. She'd made the mistake of leaving him once and couldn't believe she was even considering doing it again.

"I would never ask you to give up an opportunity to do something you love to stay here with me."

"I'd do it."

"I believe you, but I don't want you to ever regret not doing something because of me."

Besides the soft classical music playing through the speakers, silence filled the room. Each was caught up in their own thoughts.

"Maybe you can move to Milan with me," Janna blurted out.

Austin's fork stopped midway to his mouth. He looked about as shocked as she was that she'd come up with the idea. Why couldn't he take a year off and go with her?

"You're serious, aren't you?"

"Yes." She wiped her mouth with the cloth napkin. "I don't want to lose you."

"Are you saying that if I don't go with you, I'll lose *you*?"

"No. That's not what I'm saying. I just want us to discuss all possibilities before any decisions are made. And us going to Milan could be a possibility."

Disappointment settled in her joints when he said nothing. She didn't know if his silence meant that he was thinking about the idea or if it meant he wasn't interested.

Instead of pushing him for a response, she said, "Can we not talk about this anymore this evening? This is your last night here." She set down her fork and pushed out of her chair. "I'd rather spend the rest of our time together doing other things."

"Is that right?" he asked when she sat on his lap.

"Yep."

"So what did you have in mind?" He pushed her hair behind her ear and nuzzled her neck, his lips sending goose bumps up her arm.

"Maybe we can do what we did this morning, except I want to be on top."

He chuckled, the stress lines that were on his forehead moments ago gone. "I think that can be arranged."

Janna knew sharing her body with Austin would only be a temporary distraction. She also knew the moment Nelson mentioned Milan that Austin wouldn't be enthused about the assignment. Yet she had hoped they could work out a compromise. Maybe she was wrong in thinking his feelings for her were just as strong as hers were for him.

They both stood and blew out the candles, but she

couldn't stop thinking about their discussion. If Austin had asked her to forgo the opportunity, marry him and move to Atlanta, she would have said yes in a heartbeat. But he hadn't asked, and that worried her.

Chapter 15

Austin jerked awake. He glanced around the semi-darkened room, his eyes barely opened. Hearing nothing, he lowered his head back down on the sofa pillow. He wasn't sure what had awakened him out of a deep sleep and right now, he didn't care to find out.

Turning onto his side, he had no intention of getting up anytime soon. It was Saturday—at least he thought it was. After the exhausting week he'd had, he wasn't sure. Six straight twelve- to fifteen-hour workdays were enough to make a person forget his own name.

Since returning from New York, he had been on autopilot, doing any and everything to free his mind from Janna. They still talked daily, but instead of two or three times, he found excuses to take the calls once a day. She wasn't happy about that, but it couldn't be helped. He needed space. Space to think about what he wanted for his future. What he wanted with her, especially since it looked as if she was going to take the assignment in Milan.

His doorbell rang several times. Whoever was trying to get his attention was now lying on the damn bell.

Malcolm.

Austin turned onto his stomach and tried to ignore the intrusive noise, but then his brother started pounding on the door.

Damn him!

Austin leaped off the couch. Seconds later he swung the door open. "What the…" His words died on his lips. It wasn't his brother.

"You lied to me!" Janna stormed past him into the house, pulling a large suitcase behind her.

Almost afraid to find out what this was all about, Austin took his time closing the door. When he finally did, he turned to find Janna glaring at him, her hands on her hips and fire shooting out of her ears.

The last thought almost made him laugh, a good sign that he was definitely tired, or maybe it was delirium setting in.

"Every day for the last few days, I have asked if you were okay. Clearly you're not!" She waved a hand in his direction.

Austin glanced down at himself. Still in work clothes from the day before. Not only were his dress shirt and slacks wrinkled, it looked as if someone had roughed him up. A button was missing off his shirt and the tail of it was partially hanging out his pants. His belt was unfastened, barely in two or three loops, and he wore only one shoe.

"It's been a tough week, Janna." Well, for him, he thought. A good look at her revealed she was as pulled together as usual. Her face was perfectly made up and her hair hung in waves over her shoulder. The fitted white blouse she was wearing was neatly tucked into a pair of dress slacks that made her legs look even longer. And since the pants were tapered at her ankles, he could easily see her customary high heels. She looked good. She looked damn good.

When the room started spinning, he knew that if he didn't sit down soon, he would drop. Without saying anything else to Janna, he headed back to the living room.

He stretched his long frame out on the sofa, his forearm over his eyes. If he could just get a few more hours of sleep, he'd be okay. But with Janna there, that wasn't going to happen. He lunged up into a sitting position at that last thought.

"Why are you here? Is everything okay?"

"No. No, everything is not okay!" She sat on the edge of the sofa and touched her hand to the stubble on his jaw. "I'm miserable in New York and you're trying to work yourself to death. I talked with Malcolm. He told me what was going on."

Austin lay back down. "Malcolm needs to mind his own damn business."

"You are his business. He's concerned about you… and so am I. I decided I'm not going to Milan."

Austin peeked from under his arm. "Why not?"

"Because I know it would ruin what we have. Besides, I can't stand the thought of being away from you that long."

Austin shook his head. "Nah, baby, I can't let you do that."

"You're not letting me do anything." She kicked off her heels and curled up next to him. "This is what I've decided."

"Well, I'm not feeling this decision, but right now I'm too tired to argue with you." He wrapped his arm around her and placed a kiss on the side of her hair. "But this isn't over. Let me get a couple of hours of sleep, and *we* will make some decisions."

"Okay, but I have to leave here by four. I'm on my way to Miami for…"

Austin tried staying awake, but his eyes grew heavy. As long as his baby was in his arms, all was well with the world.

Hours later, Austin exited his bedroom feeling like a new man. After more sleep and a long, hot shower, he was in a better frame of mind to talk with Janna.

When he smelled something burning, he flew down the stairs. The smoke detector erupted the moment he stepped in the kitchen.

"Babe, what are you doing?" He hurried across the kitchen and turned the stove off. He placed the smoking skillet in the sink.

"I was trying to make you a grilled cheese sandwich, but it didn't turn out too good." She bit her bottom lip and pushed a plate over to him. The charred item could have been a sandwich, but had she not told him what it was, he would have thought it was charcoal.

He chuckled and pulled her into his arms, kissing her. "Thank you, but I think it'll be safer if I continue doing the cooking in this relationship."

Over a light lunch of grilled cheese and salad, they talked more about Milan.

"I don't know, Austin. You're making this plan sound easier than I think it would be."

"Do you want to go, Janna?"

She hesitated and stared down into her lap. He knew the answer before he'd asked the question.

"Yes," she finally said. "But—"

"I don't want you to have any regrets if you don't go for it. Who knows what this can do for your career? You can't pass up this assignment." He didn't even want to think about what would have happened if she hadn't jumped at the chance to go to Milan at sixteen. Because of that decision back then, she was doing what she was born to do. There was no way he would stand in her way now.

"I'm not going to Milan unless you go with me."

"Baby, I can't just pick up my life as easily as you can. I have too many people depending on me. It's for one year. Like Nelson said, it's a once-in-a-lifetime opportunity, and then there's Phoenix. You'll get a chance to know her better and work with her. Something you recently said you'd like to do."

Janna shook her head. "I don't want to lose you like last time."

"You won't. Besides, last time was different. This plan will work if we want it to."

"But we'll only see each other once a month."

"And holidays."

She huffed and stood suddenly, taking her plate to the sink. "That's not enough," she said quietly, her back to him. "I want more."

He wanted more, too. He wanted nothing more than to make her his wife, move her to Atlanta and raise a family. But he had to think about her career, something she loved and was meant to do. It wasn't the right time to propose.

Janna stared out her living room window that overlooked Central Park, listening to her sisters on the telephone. She had called them to talk about her relocation to Milan and get their opinion regarding Austin.

"To me, Janna doesn't seem as excited about this assignment like others, Iris. Why push her to take it?" Macy asked.

"Because it's a great opportunity. Since Austin is okay with it and they've worked out a plan to continue seeing each other, why not go?"

Janna listened as they went back and forth discussing her life as if she weren't on the call. Since her impromptu trip to Atlanta a week ago, she hadn't been able to stop thinking about what she and Austin had decided. Then while he was visiting her this past weekend, he'd made it sound as if the year would go by fast, that they would be able to see each other enough. But seeing him once or twice a month wasn't enough now, and it definitely wouldn't be if she went to Milan.

"Janna, why aren't you saying anything?" Iris asked, pulling her back into the conversation.

"I was just hearing what you guys had to say."

"During the past half an hour, there's one question we haven't asked," Macy said. "Janna, what do you want?"

What do I want? What do I really want?

"I want to marry Austin, have a family and a career. I want what we agreed to back in high school," she said quietly, as if talking to herself.

For the first time during the call, silence filled the phone line. Janna was a little surprised by her response, and apparently so were her sisters.

"I don't think I have *ever* heard you mention wanting to get married and have a family," Iris said, her tone wistful.

"Me either," Macy added, sounding just as shocked. "Does Austin know you want that?"

Janna hesitated. She assumed he did, but the more she thought about it, the more she realized they hadn't really talked specifically about marriage and children since reuniting.

How would he know if I haven't told him?

Chapter 16

Austin turned onto the street where his parents lived, exhausted from a whirlwind trip to New York. This time he had only stayed two days, knowing he needed to be back in the office this morning at 6 a.m. Returning very late last night, he'd barely slept before his alarm clock started blaring. To say he was tired would be an understatement. It didn't help knowing Janna was planning to leave the country soon.

The closer it got to October 15, the more anxious Austin got. Janna wanted to get to Milan a few weeks early in order to get settled before the assignment started. Now that she was more excited about the idea of going to Milan and working with Phoenix, he was a wreck, and she hadn't even left the country yet.

Austin walked into his parents' home, feeling as if

he'd been dragged through a minefield, his thoughts weighing him down. He had to get himself together. Distracted by his relationship issues, he wasn't on top of his game at work and those around him were noticing.

"Austin, is that you?" his father called from some-where in the back of the house.

"Yeah, it's me." He stuffed his keys into his pockets and headed to where his father's voice came from. He stopped short at the door to their home office. "What's going on? I got your voice message."

"Come in, son," his mother said, looking as if she hadn't slept in days. Fear gripped him immediately see-ing her that way, his father hovering nearby.

"Is everything okay?" Austin slid one of the guest chairs from next to the desk over to the sofa where his parents were sitting. "What's happened?" Every horri-ble thought conceivable ran rampant through his mind. He couldn't take any more bad news. At work, they had lost a bid on a project that they'd thought for sure they'd won, and then one of their computer servers crashed.

"Now can you tell me what's going on?" his father asked Sheila and then turned his attention to Austin. "She's been acting strange for the last couple of days, claiming that there was something she needed to tell you."

"What is it, Mom?"

She handed him a white, letter-sized envelope. He glanced at the information on the front of it. His breath hitched and a sudden tingling on the back of his neck sent his pulse raising.

The envelope, addressed to him, had their old Edison, New Jersey, address. But it was the sender's information that had his heartbeat galloping. Then he noticed the postmark.

Janna's letter.

A sick feeling churned in his gut when he turned the envelope over and saw it had been opened. He didn't speak. He didn't ask his parents the question that he already thought he knew the answer to. Instead, he pulled the letter out, and his hands shook slightly at the sight of a faded red lip print on the outside.

Janna. She used to always wear a tinted lip-gloss while they were dating, strawberry flavored. She must have kissed the letter after folding it.

Austin's chest tightened with emotion. He unfolded the letter and read:

Dear Austin,

By the time you get this letter I'll be in Milan. I know you're wondering why. It's a long story that I can't wait to tell you about.

Since you're on the cruise with your family, I couldn't reach you. Hope it was fun and I can't wait to hear about it.

I'm sorry I couldn't tell you about Milan before I made my decision. Everything happened so fast, but I have a modeling opportunity. It's exciting and scary at the same time. I had to leave immediately; otherwise I would have waited and talked to you first. I don't have a telephone number for where I'll be, but here is my new manager's number in New York. His name is Nelson. I'm not sure how long it'll take to get a telephone in Milan, but call him to reach me.

I don't have time to write all of the details about the modeling job, but when you call me, I'll tell you everything.

I love you so much. Please don't be disappointed in me. I know we have plans to marry in a few years. I can't wait to marry you, but I had to give modeling a shot in the meantime.

This might sound selfish, but can you come to Milan with me? I know you have already decided on a college, but maybe you can start here and finish in the US. I can send you the money for the move with my first check. Don't say no. Think about it.

I already miss you and I haven't even left yet. Please call me when you get this letter.
I love you,
Janna

Austin refolded the letter and stuffed it back into the envelope. He blew out the breath that he'd been holding while reading it.

"Where did this come from?" he finally asked his parents, his voice calmer than he felt.

"I had it," his mother said, wiping her eyes.

Austin didn't know how long he sat there staring at her, anger quickly building.

"*You* had the letter?" he yelled, catching everyone off guard.

"Hey! Lower your tone, young man. You can be

upset, but I won't have you raising your voice at your mother," Patrick said.

"How could you? How could you not give me this? You knew how I felt about her! You knew better than anyone." He leaped up, the letter in his hand.

"Sheila, why didn't you give him the letter?"

She dabbed at the tears that were rolling down her cheeks faster than she could catch them. Austin was having a hard time feeling sympathy for her. A mix of shock, hurt and anger rolled into one raged through his veins.

"I didn't find it right away. I'm not sure how long it was at the house in New Jersey, but I found it in a magazine about a month after Janna left."

"And why didn't you give it to Austin when you found it?"

"At the time, I thought I was doing what was best for both of you." Her teary eyes watched Austin. She cried harder and Austin hated to see his mother like this, but he couldn't believe she had done this to him. "When I saw that Janna wanted you to come to Milan with her... I had to intervene."

"What?"

"Austin, honey, I absolutely adore Janna. Always have. But I couldn't let you both throw away your lives for a high school crush."

"It was more than that!" Austin yelled but caught sight of his father's warning glare. He remained quiet until he could rein in his temper. "I loved Janna with everything in me. And yes, I probably would have given up my scholarships to be with her. Withholding this letter was not your call. You had no right."

"I had every right," she said through gritted teeth and stood slowly. "You are my son and at the time you were just a child."

"I was old enough to make my own decisions."

"You were still *my* child. Your father and I have always wanted what was best for you boys. You had a promising future ahead of you with multiple scholarships. I couldn't let you throw that away."

"I can't believe it." He paced the length of the room. Janna had been telling the truth about the letter. *God, all this time.* His mind flashed back to how he'd treated her when they ran into each other at the bakery…and then at the fundraiser.

He glanced at the envelope in his hand. She had loved him. She really did love him and she'd wanted to marry him.

Patrick walked over and laid his hand on Austin's shoulder. "There are times when good people make bad decisions."

In his head, Austin knew that, but in his heart, he wasn't trying to hear it.

When his mother walked over, he said, "Thanks for finally giving me the letter. It clears up some things."

"Honey, I'm so sorry. I hope that you can one day find it in your heart to forgive me."

Austin accepted the hug she gave him, but he had to get out of there. He couldn't breathe.

"I have to go." He headed to the door.

"Maybe you shouldn't leave like this." His father caught up to him. "Where are you going?"

"I...I'm not sure. I just..." He stopped and turned to his father, knowing exactly what he had to do. "I'm going back to New York."

Austin rushed home to throw a few things in a bag, including the velvet box that had been traveling back and forth with him over the past few weeks. He didn't pack much. All he wanted was to get to Janna. He caught the first flight out.

It was almost 10 p.m. when he arrived at her apartment. He dug out the keys that she'd given him, but before he could unlock the door, it swung open.

Janna gasped, her hand hovering over her chest. "You scared me. Austin, what are you doing here? I thought you were back in Atlanta."

Austin noticed her luggage sitting just inside the door. "I forgot something."

She tilted her head and frowned. "What'd you forget?"

"You. I forgot you." He stepped to her and before she could utter a word, he braced her face between his hands and devoured her lips. There was no way he could continue living without seeing her on a regular basis. And there was no way in hell he was letting her leave him again.

He slowly lifted his head and stared into dazed eyes.

"Wow. That was nice." Janna swiped her tongue across her upper lip.

He grinned and kissed her again before finally pulling away. He stepped into the apartment and nodded to the luggage.

"Where are you going? I thought you didn't leave for your shoot in Chicago for another couple of days."

"That was the plan, but I forgot something, too."

"What do you mean?"

"I was on my way to Atlanta. When you were here this weekend, I forgot to tell you that I can't live without you. If it means breaking my contract, giving up Milan and even modeling, I'm prepared to do that. I want the life I have always dreamed of...with you."

A slow smile spread across Austin's mouth at her words and Janna couldn't stop the grin from covering her lips. She couldn't believe he was there and she'd finally said what she should have said months ago.

"Come with me." Austin held her hand and led her to the living room. He didn't stop until they were in front of the windows.

She glanced out into the dark, lights bouncing off nearby buildings. Not knowing what she was supposed to be looking at, she turned back to Austin.

"What am I..." She stopped speaking and placed her hands over her mouth when Austin went down on one knee.

"I have loved you since you were sixteen and though I thought I would be doing this way before now—officially—I can't go another day without asking...will you marry me?"

Tears blurred her vision and she bobbed her head up and down like a bobblehead toy.

"Yes! Oh, yes, I will definitely marry you!" She lunged into his arms, almost toppling them both over.

Austin laughed and placed the gorgeous diamond on her finger. Standing, he said, "There's one condition."

"Anything."

"You have to marry me within the next three weeks."

Janna's eyebrows creased with confusion. "I'd be willing to do it right now, but what happens in three weeks?"

"I want us to be married before we go to Milan."

For a moment, she was too stunned to speak, afraid she hadn't heard him correctly.

"Wha— *We*?"

Austin chuckled and pulled her into his arms. "Yes, we."

He told her about the letter and the conversation with his parents. Janna's heart hurt for his mother. She knew how close Sheila and Austin were and prayed that he could forgive her. Had Janna been in his mother's shoes, she might have done the same thing.

"Baby, I hate that so many situations kept us apart," Austin said, caressing her cheek. "I need you to know that I love you more than I ever thought I could love another human being."

"Oh, Austin, I love you, too, but are you sure you can go with me?"

"The first time you asked me to go with you ten years ago, the decision was taken out of my hands before I even knew about the invite. There is no way I'm going to pass up another opportunity. Besides, from now on, I'm going wherever my wife goes."

Epilogue

Two and a half weeks later

Janna giggled as Austin grabbed her hand and pulled her across the backyard to his workshop. They were getting married the next day and her sisters had insisted on keeping her and Austin apart the night before the ceremony. Supposedly it would make the wedding night that much more special. As far as Janna was concerned, every night with him was special.

Once she and Austin were safely inside, he locked the door and pulled her into his arms.

"That wasn't as hard as I thought it would be," he murmured against her lips. "Your sisters have been guarding you like you're some type of princess or something."

"Didn't I tell you? I am a princess."

"Yeah, sure," he mumbled against her neck. His soft kisses sent goose bumps traveling down her arms.

Squirming under his touch, Janna said, "Phoenix is considered the queen of the big screen. So as her daughter, that automatically makes me a princess."

Austin slowly lifted his head and met Janna's gaze. She knew what he was thinking. She was claiming Phoenix as her mother.

"She'll never be my mama, but she is my mother. I can finally say that without bile rising up in my throat." She chuckled and walked over to the sofa.

"Well, that's progress. I guess planning the wedding with her, you've had a chance to get to know her better." Austin sat next to her and Janna's gaze zoned in on the small, beautifully wrapped box he set on the coffee table.

"Yeah, she's actually pretty cool. As a matter of fact, she reminds me of myself. Scary, huh?" They both laughed. "I'm dying to know what's in the box."

"Something for you."

She rubbed her hands together and then accepted the box from him. "You know I love surprises." She quickly ripped off the paper and lifted the lid, surprised to see a set of keys.

"Hmm, what are these to?" she asked excitedly. She already had keys to his home.

"When thinking about a wedding gift for my future wife, I had the hardest time finding something for the person who has everything."

"Austin, you didn't have to get me anything. Marrying you is all I need."

"You might think differently when I tell you what those keys are to."

"Okay, tell me!"

"Those will open the doors to your first Precious Home building for kids who have aged out of foster care." He handed her a portfolio of photos. "I'm thinking we can turn the space into a homelike environment, where each youth will have their own bedroom and bath suite."

"Oh, Austin." She sat stunned as she went through the portfolio, looking at pictures of the empty building, as well as the area around the home. The three-story brick mansion was perfect for what she had in mind for the nonprofit.

"Once we're done with the renovations, the space will include a large eat-in kitchen and a TV room. Oh, and it's located in Edison. I know you said you wanted to start with three buildings, one there, one in New York and one in Atlanta. Well, you can scratch one off your list."

"This is…this is too much."

"Nothing is too much for my future wife."

She glanced up and the love she saw brimming in his eyes almost made her cry. There were days when she still couldn't believe she was marrying the only man she'd ever loved.

"I can hardly wait to be your wife."

The next day, Janna stood in the full-length mirror, awed by the beauty of her custom-made wedding gown. Sure, she had modeled hundreds of dresses in her lifetime, but as far as she was concerned, none were exquisite as hers. The bodice, adorned with Swarovski crystals, had an empire waist that flared out into a full, heavily beaded lace skirt.

Butterflies fluttered around in her stomach. She still couldn't believe she was marrying Austin. When Phoenix had insisted on helping with the preparations, she had told her that she didn't need a big wedding and a gorgeous gown to marry Austin. Had he been interested, she would have been just as happy marrying him in jeans and a T-shirt in Vegas. He wasn't having that. They'd both agreed that neither of them wanted anything huge, but Austin insisted that she get the wedding she'd dreamed about as a teen.

Janna turned from the mirror, smiling at how quickly they'd been able to pull their wedding together. Their mothers and her sisters were determined to make this a special day for her and Austin. As an A-list actress, Phoenix had a long reach when it came to everything from caterers to entertainment. Janna was still a little hesitant about letting her get too close, but Phoenix had proven that she wasn't trying to replace Mama Adel. She just wanted to have Janna in her life in any capacity that Janna was willing to allow.

The wedding was being held in Nash and Iris's backyard. Their new home was perfect since it offered the seclusion Janna wanted. But even with tons of security, the paparazzi were still hanging out by the front gates in hopes of getting photos of the festivities.

"Okay, it's time." Macy rushed into the guest room that Janna was using, followed by Iris, Tania and Mama

Adel. Her sisters and niece looked perfect in their slate-gray bridesmaid dresses.

"Sweetheart, you look absolutely stunning," her mother said, gripping Janna's hands, her smile as warm as usual. "I would say that I hope Austin knows what he's getting, but I have a feeling he does. Though I regret not taking your feelings for him more seriously years ago, I know that God's timing is always best. He brought you two back together once you both had accomplished your individual goals, and I know your union will be all the more blessed."

Tears pricked the backs of Janna's eyes as she struggled to keep them at bay. She had always thought that her mother was one of the wisest people she'd ever known.

"Thank you, Mama, for loving me and supporting my dreams. Though I'm not saying that our love wouldn't have eventually gotten Austin and me to this point, you might be right about one thing. I know that by us going our separate ways and pursuing our dreams, we're able to bring so much more to our marriage." She accepted the hug from her mother and whispered in her ear, "Thank you for your unconditional love."

Mama Adel gave her a squeeze before releasing her. "I can't believe my baby is getting married," she sobbed.

"Aw, Mama, don't start," Macy said, wrapping her arm around their mother's shoulders. "You're going to have Janna crying and then—"

"Too late," Iris said as she snatched up some tissue and started dabbing at Janna's eyes, careful not to ruin her makeup. "I knew I shouldn't have let her come in here."

Janna laughed through her tears as Iris fussed over her.

"Come on, Grandma," Tania said, "let's go and find your seat."

"Okay, it's time." Phoenix hurried into the room, followed by Patrick Reynolds, who was walking Janna down the aisle. "You look absolutely gorgeous," Phoenix said.

"Thank you." Janna accepted a hug from her. "And thank you for everything you've done to make this happen in such a short amount of time."

"It was the least I could do. Thank you for letting me be a part of your special day. It means everything to me." Phoenix squeezed her hand, looking as if she were going to start crying.

"Okay, let's get this show on the road." Macy gently moved Phoenix away, knowing that tears were about to start again.

"Are you ready, sweetheart?" Mr. Reynolds asked.

"Yes." Janna looped her arm through his, feeling a little giddy that she was about to get the father she had always yearned for. "Thank you for walking me down the aisle."

"The pleasure is all mine." He placed a kiss on her cheek and guided her out of the room.

Austin glanced around the enormous backyard, taking in all of the decor and flowers. Everything had turned out even better than he expected. He and Janna hadn't given their families much notice, but they'd pulled everything together in record time. And while they planned the wedding, he took care of things at his office. He would remain CFO of Reynolds Development, but most of his work would be done remotely with the help of his financial team.

Austin shook a few of their guests' hands as he made his way down the makeshift aisle. Even though he and Janna had both agreed that they only wanted immediate family and close friends in attendance, they'd had a hard time keeping the guest list to a hundred people. They would have a big reception and invite everyone they knew after they returned from Milan, to celebrate their first anniversary.

He stopped at the front row of chairs, where his mother was sitting.

"Hey, Mom." Austin sat in his father's seat for a moment. "How's it going?"

"Everything is incredible. I can't believe how quickly they were able to transform the yard." She looked up and patted his cheek. "Are you ready for your big day?"

"Definitely." He grinned, still pinching himself that this was really happening. A few days after he'd proposed to Janna, he and his mother had made amends. He might have been hurt by her actions, but he understood why she'd felt she had to withhold the letter. He also realized later that seeing the letter gave him the push needed to do what he should have done sooner— ask Janna to marry him.

His mother squeezed his hand. "I am so happy for you and Janna. I wish you both many, many wonderful years together."

"Thanks, Mom. Thanks for everything." He kissed her on the cheek. "I love you."

"I love you, too, son. And feel free to start working on my grandkids right away."

Austin laughed and stood. "I'll keep that in mind."

"All right, you ready to do this, man?" Malcolm, his best man, clapped him on the shoulder.

"More than ready."

They walked up to the wedding arbor and got in place.

"It's showtime," his brother said next to him.

As soon as the music started, the wedding party marched in. Of course the kids stole the show. Macy and Derek's son, Jason, pulled a decorated white wagon down the aisle. In the wagon were his one-year-old sister, Amber, who was the flower girl, and Iris and Nash's twin boys, Stephen and Trevon, the ring bearers. Before Austin knew it, it was time for Janna's entry.

Despite Mama Adel's objection, Janna had chosen the song "I'll Always Love You" by Taylor Dayne instead of the wedding march as her processional.

Austin readied himself when the music started, but nothing could prepare him for the vision of loveliness who stepped out of the house. Words could not describe the emotions welling up inside him at the sight of her.

"You all right, bro?" Malcolm nudged him, humor in his voice. "I'll brace myself to catch you just in case you faint."

Austin shook his head and smiled. Not even Malcolm could rattle him today. It felt as if he had waited a lifetime for this moment, and he couldn't wait to make

Janna his wife. Happy that the ceremony would be short and sweet, he was looking forward to getting her alone and out of that dress.

Fifteen minutes later, the minister said, "You may now kiss the bride."

Austin stepped forward and cupped her face within his hands, staring into her eyes. When he lowered his head and touched her lips with his, it was as if he had come home. Their life had come full circle and she was finally his. He kissed with everything in him and she matched him stroke for stroke. He was so caught up in the moment, he would have forgotten they had an audience until cheers and whistles went up around them.

He lifted his head and smiled at his beautiful wife. "I will always love you."

"And I'll always love you."

* * * * *

Prepare to be swept away as two couples embark on an odyssey of secret longings and scorching desires...

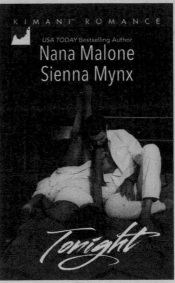

USA TODAY Bestselling Author
Nana Malone
Sienna Mynx

CITY OF SIN by Nana Malone: A weekend at Las Vegas's Decadence Hotel is strictly business for analyst Synthia Michaels. Until her rival for a major account—gorgeous, blue-eyed Tristan Dawson—shows her just how irresistible a bad boy can be...

SHIPWRECKED by Sienna Mynx: Professor Deja Jones still fantasizes about the mind-blowing kiss she shared with Jon Hendrix. Now a celebration on his family's private island brings her face-to-face once again with the enticingly sexy sports agent!

Available April 2016!

REQUEST YOUR FREE BOOKS!

2 FREE NOVELS PLUS 2 *FREE GIFTS!*

KIMANI™ ROMANCE

Love's ultimate destination!

KROM15

Turn your love of reading into rewards you'll love with
Harlequin My Rewards

**Join for FREE today at
www.HarlequinMyRewards.com**

Earn **FREE BOOKS** of your choice.

Experience **EXCLUSIVE OFFERS** and contests.

Enjoy **BOOK RECOMMENDATIONS**
selected just for you.

PLUS! Sign up now
and get **500** points
right away!

Earn
FREE
REWARDS
HarlequinMyRewards.com
Join
Today!

MYR16R

SPECIAL EXCERPT FROM

ⒽHARLEQUIN®

KIMANI
ROMANCE

*After dumping her controlling fiancé, Chey Rodgers is
ready to live her life. Step one is moving to New York to
complete her degree—getting snowed in with a sensual
stranger isn't part of the plan! Successful attorney
Hunter Barrington has one semester to succeed as a
professor at his alma mater. He's put to the test when the
sultry beauty who shared his bed at a ski resort reappears
in his classroom. Will Hunter and Chey be able to avoid
scandal and attain their dreams of each other?*

Read on for a sneak peek at
HIS LOVE LESSON, the next exciting installment of
Nicki Night's
THE BARRINGTON BROTHERS *series!*

"Nice seeing you again…um…?" She pretended to forget
his name.

"Hunter," he interjected and held his hand out once again.

Chey shook it and that same feeling from before
returned—a slight flutter in her belly.

"Well—" she cleared her throat "—have a good night.
I guess I'll see you around."

"I'm sure. Probably right here in the same spot."
He chuckled.

"Oh. Sorry," Chey said for lack of anything better. "Good
night," she said again.

Chey didn't stop walking until she reached her villa. She pushed the door open, then quickly closed it behind her and leaned her back against it. Why was her heart beating so fast? Why was she flustered? Chey had carefully planned out her day and now that she'd had another encounter with the stranger—Hunter—she was mentally off balance.

Shaking off the feeling that had attached itself to her from the moment he touched her hand again, Chey headed to the first bedroom and pulled out her laptop. She decided to work on her novel. She booted up her computer and started reading through the last chapter she'd written. Every time she read the male character's lines, she imagined Hunter's voice, until finally she put the laptop aside and burst out laughing.

Chey lay back on the comfortable bed and savored the firmness of the mattress as it seemed to mold itself to her body. A vision of Hunter sleeping uneasily in that chair in the lobby popped into her mind. Chey closed her eyes tight in an attempt to rid herself of thoughts of him. She worked at this for some time before rising from the bed, bundling up and heading back to the main reception area to find Hunter, who was now "resting" in a new chair.

"You can have the second room in my villa on one condition."

Don't miss
HIS LOVE LESSON by Nicki Night,
available May 2016 wherever
Harlequin® Kimani Romance™
books and ebooks are sold.

Copyright © 2016 by Renee Daniel Flagler